RED
AND THE
RESTORER

RED ORIGINS
BOOK THREE

KENDRAI MEEKS

ONE

Never did Gunda Faust allow grays to streak outwardly across the bold colors of her declarations. Oh, in her heart, her spirit often rebelled against the injuries her position forced upon those around her, but not even her own husband had heard her doubts regarding their eldest daughter. Helga did claim many traits that would make her a powerful leader: intelligence, cunning, determination, even beauty... But woven into the cord of her demeanor ran an undeniable thread of sadism. Gunda would be the last to propose violence was without place in the policing of wolves, but extreme acts should be born of extreme circumstances. Helga lusted for blood not to nourish power, but to quench a thirst for pain.

She'd managed to rule the wolves, but in short order, she'd lose her family's loyalty, and where would that leave things? All her children in the ground, that's where. Gunda shuddered when she thought of any of her progeny coming to violent ends. A matron demanded respect and obeisance, but that didn't mean she held no love for her children. Gunda treasured all five, from fierce Helga to reserved Gerwalta.

And then the news came from Venice: Gerwalta could fly. By the traditions of their kind, it was a sign that it was the youngest child, not the eldest, who would follow Gunda unto the throne. Helga wouldn't cede for tradition's sake, however. Her youngest, so often overlooked, would now find herself on the sharpened end of her eldest sister's sword. Perhaps the wolfsretter of the House of Night to whom Gerwalta had betrothed herself would help keep her from harm. It wasn't the match Gunda would've chosen, but it was a good match for a child she suspected would be reluctant to sink to cruelty.

A knock on the door pulled the Matron from her reverie.

"Enter."

Helga's head poked through the chamber door, bringing Gunda to her feet. "What? What has happened?"

When the door swung farther, revealing Gerwalta's intended, Mehmet, in Helga's wake, the Matron knew.

"She refuses to enter the tent." Gunda nodded in the shadow of her own presumption as the other two crept in. "Never fear, Herr Siyah, nerves about the joining aren't uncommon and quickly remedied. I'll find my erstwhile daughter directly and assure that she performs her marital duties posthaste."

The two young people exchanged a look of confusion.

Gunda arrested herself on the spot. "There is something more."

Helga looked to her clenched hands. "Yes, Gerwalta didn't claim her bridegroom, but the situation is more dire than nerves. What I mean to say is..."

The Ottoman wolfsretter assumed the rest. "It appears she has betrayed our vows and your clan, Matron," he announced. "She has run into the arms of the königswolf."

The news hit Gunda in the gut and threw her off balance. "Impossible. No wolfsretter of the House of Red would do such a thing."

"Yet, it appears to be so," Helga resumed. "No one in the schloss has seen Gerwalta for nearly an hour. Maximillian just returned from the packlands, reporting that the königswolf is also unaccounted for."

"But that doesn't mean... It's not as though Gerwalta would..."

Or would she? Truth be told, Gunda had suspected some festering secret behind her daughter's eyes. When Gerwalta had returned from Venice proclaiming she'd arranged her own marriage, Gunda had surmised that her youngest had pulled an excellent coup, working some secret conspiracy. Could it really be the secret she'd been hiding was that she was in love with a lupine?

Each of the Matron's knuckles cracked in succession as her hands tightened into fists. "Find them."

Both Mehmet and Helga dipped their heads, the latter saying, "And what shall we do with them?"

"Bring them both before me in chains," Gunda declared. "He in silver, she in iron. I'll have the truth of it from their own mouths."

Mehmet stepped forward. "Matron Faust, if I may? You are entertaining a great many guests, and it is possible that Gerwalta hasn't committed any act of the flesh with the lupine. I'd suggest a small party of men for this mission. Perhaps this can be contained silently, and men will not be missed as much from the festivities. It may still be possible to seal our union and merely punish the wolf without any inside the grounds being any the wiser tonight."

She chewed on that a moment, discerning the taste. "Yes, perhaps. Helga, send the men, your brother included. My order otherwise stands but advise them to be discreet upon their return. Once I have the truth of it, I'll decide how to proceed."

TWO

Pulling on Andreas's hand had as much effect as yelling at the wind. There was no arresting him. Unless she wanted to cause him injury.

Honestly, breaking one of his legs became more tempting by the moment.

"Andreas, stop! I cannot go before the pack like this. I haven't any clothing!"

That at least made him slow a fraction as he glanced back at her over his shoulder. "Yes, and I approve wholeheartedly."

"You approve?" Enough of this foolery. She wouldn't cede their lives on the altar of his amusement. Gerwalta sped her steps, placing herself between him and the path back to the pack's farmstead, her arms stretched out wide. "What part of 'we need to run with haste for our very lives' didn't you grasp? We haven't time to visit the pack for a social farewell."

At last, he stopped. Andreas fixed her with feasting eyes, raking over the contours of her unclad form. "Exquisite."

She fell in on herself, attempting to cover her treasures. "You may be a wolf, Andreas Barron, but you are still such a man."

"It is no sin for one to appreciate the beauty of his mate."

"It is if it comes at the cost of her life." She pressed on. "That Helga hasn't already arrived is a slim blessing. I love you. I've given myself to you, but will you treat that so gallantly as not to heed my warning?"

He stepped forward, closing the space between them. At first, Gerwalta thought he may mean to take her again—he'd already attempted once. Instead, Andreas's gaze softened. He took up her hands in his, raising them to his mouth to kiss the back of her knuckles.

"Love, hear me," he begged. "I am the königswolf. If I leave my pack without proper ceremony, the consequences for them will be manifold."

"You were prepared to leave them without ceremony when we were in Venice," Gerwalta argued.

"Then I had already been away from them for nearly two moons. A third would snap my tether with them, letting them decide upon a new king. But now..."

"If you left, there would be no one to represent them against the Matron." Gerwalta cut him off. His sad eyes told her she'd surmised the consequences. "There needs be a new king ere we depart. But, Andreas, in our current circumstances, that can happen only if one of your pack defeats you in battle. Your pack loves you. None would dare."

"Do you forget so quickly, love?" he asked. "There is a new packling, one who harbors quite a dislike for me."

"But to leave him in charge against my family would... He'll drive them into silver swords for certain!"

Andreas turned back towards the village. "Once Gerhart is king, a king's honor will comply him to do what is in the best interest of the pack. He'll protect them."

"And if he doesn't?"

Despair contorted the beautiful brow of her beloved. "Then we are all dead."

THREE

Andreas met Wilhelm's eyes across the shorn field. A momentary smile faded as Gerwalta stepped from the tree line in his wake.

Wilhelm dropped his pitchfork and stumbled forward. The sheep, awaking with the dawn, would have to wait for their morning meal. Andreas hesitated, wondering what he would say when they were close enough for words. Many times he'd imagined a foggy future in which his beloved would be his mate and mother of his pups, dreamed of their bliss and resilience in the face of adversity to their coupling, but he'd never anticipated the ignition of the battle they were sure to wage. Now, staring down its nose, he wasn't sure how to confront the beast of their reality.

Whatever the next few minutes held, they were only the first of the forever in which they'd always be in violation of not only Dark One ways, but of their very nature. If Andreas couldn't gain the understanding of his own pack—of his own second—what hope did they have?

Gerwalta, clutching the edge of her conjured red cloak in an effort to conceal her nudity, drew to a stop at his side.

"He is wondering if I am stalking you. Quickly, take my hand."

Andreas didn't allow his gaze to break from his second's as he complied. "There is such hate in his eyes."

"It is for me, not you," Gerwalta assured him. "We should expect nothing less."

"We should hope for so much more." Andreas licked his lips. "Whatever happens, know that you are my priority. I'll protect you."

She pulled his hands to her lips, even as it forced some view of her flesh beneath. "I vow the same."

By the time the two parties had closed the distance, Wilhelm boiled. "Mein könig? What goes on here?"

So few words, but what they said was so much more. They spoke of confusion, anger, betrayal, desperation. Heartbreak.

Abandonment.

Andreas assumed the confident mask of the ruler. "Wilhelm, gather the pack."

"You cannot possibly mean to say that—"

"Wilhelm!" Andreas more growled than spoke. The wolf raged within him, a command now, not a request. His second would have only two choices: comply or defect. "Now say I."

Forever gathered in a dew drop as Andreas waited. Finally, Wilhelm acquiesced. With a pivot, the lupine within him took control, letting out a high, wallowing howl. Soon enough, the others began to come into view, moving with haste from whatever daybreak errand they'd been about. Some still carried the implements of their tasks. A washboard, a basket of eggs, a butchering knife...

His pack... He loved them each. Some he'd grown up with. Some, grown older under. Some had grown under him. To be their könig had been his joy, his privilege. But now, he'd be their greatest regret.

"I have an announcement." He resumed hold of Gerwalta's hand, pulling his beloved under his wing. "I've chosen my mate, and it is she."

Several of them flinched. Others looked ill. A mother with her young pup in her arms covered the boy's ears, as though the act would keep the evil of the world from soaking his thoughts.

"Mein könig, you cannot be serious." Wilhelm voiced that which Andreas knew they all thought. "She is one of them."

"She was one of them," Andreas declared. "And now, she is my mate."

As he'd predicted, the Wehr pack defector stepped forward. "I knew it would come to this, and now, Andreas Barron's arrogance and betrayal to the pack will cost us all." Gerhart turned to the others, addressing his words to them. "You know their law: a wolf who tussles with a wolfsretter is subject to death. And as it is our king who has committed the crime, we all will bear the punishment, all because he took satisfaction up some red bitch's skirt."

"How dare you!" Gerwalta was out of Andreas's grip and charging Gerhart ere he could recall her, her finger drilling into the lupine's chest, her nakedness forgotten. "How dare you betray your fealty to the wolf who spared your life."

"You mean when you wanted to kill me?" Gerhart pushed right back, but Gerwalta didn't falter. Even now, with daggers being thrown her way from the glare of every wolf, his love stood firm.

It was an accusation for certes, but one she wouldn't eschew. "Yes, when I wanted to kill you. You owe him your breath, and you use it to speak ill against him."

Wilhelm's mate Lisi, came between them. "The matter of who owes who what is of little consequence," she said. "You may love Andreas, and if he has mated you, the same is true for him. But Gerhart is right, it matters not. Your mother will use this as an excuse to bring down harsh judgement on us all, for they'll come for Andreas, and we, his pack, will be duty bound to fight for him."

"Not if I am no longer king."

Wilhelm swung about. "Sire, you don't mean to have one of us challenge you?"

"I do, and I expect it immediately. According to my mate, Helga implied a mission to either corrupt or destroy me. Gerwalta had come to warn me."

He let them stitch together the threads of the implied: and so my solution was to stop playing lovers' games and make her my mate, firm and true. There was no call to pour salt upon their wounds.

"Helga won't come alone. A team requires coordination, planning, time. Perhaps even the Red Matron readies herself for my destruction and yours as I speak. I am your king, and as such, it is my duty to protect you from all dangers, even if the source of that danger is me. One of you must challenge me, and once defeated in battle, exile me so that the Reds shall have no cause to exact vengeance on you."

Suddenly, Gerwalta's eyes went wide. She'd thought through the ramifications of his intentions then. "But Andreas, without a pack, you'll go mad."

"Not immediately. I'll have three moons for us to find a new pack."

"And who will take in an exiled king with a wolfsretter whore for a mate?"

Andreas would give credit to Gerhart that he didn't flinch as the back of Gerwalta's hand connected with his chin. Perfect. It would raise the wolf's ire all the more, playing right into Andreas's plan.

"As a dark one, I am many accursed things, but I am no whore. I've taken but one man to my bed, and it is and will ever be only your king."

Andreas had chosen his mate well. She was more shewolf in spirit than any lupine he'd encountered. Pride burned in his chest as he stepped forward, peeling off the clothes he'd only just put back on in the woods not a half hour before. "One of you will challenge me, by god, for it is your only path to salvation. Now, step forward, or I will demand—"

"I challenge!" Gerhart stepped into his role just in the nick of time. The scrappy, southern wolf stepped forward, teeth bared even in his layman form. He mirrored the king, undoing his clothing, preparing for battle. "You are an embarrassment of a wolf and a sham of a king, and it will be my honor to assume your mantle."

No sooner were the two ready to bare fangs and assume their fur than they all heard it: a battle horn from the mountain.

Andreas turned to Lisi. "My last orders as king are these: first, and with much haste, clothe my bride. Second, secure the pups and what shewolves can be obligated beyond their care, prepare a defense."

Lisi looked for a moment as though she may refuse, perhaps even argue, but all knew that any delay invited death going forward.

"Yes, my king." Lisi curtsied, took Gerwalta by the wrist, and escorted the children and the shewolves to the farmhouse.

Only the men remained.

Andreas turned out his hands, cracking his knuckles. "Wince I am defeated, you must make haste to exile me and let the Reds know I am no longer of the pack."

"Don't forfeit, Andreas," Wilhelm said, "or the transfer of kingship won't take."

He knew this. It wasn't a simple thing to become königswolf. To mock battle wouldn't do. Andreas could also not merely cede. Gerhart must defeat him.

Andreas gave one last solemn nod. "I won't yield, but for the sake of every member of this pack, Gerhart, you had better force me to my surrender with great urgency."

The two wolves cried out as they let their power take them, making fur of what had been flesh and fang of what had been jaw. The hulking forms stared at the each other, unmoving save for the curl of their lips over long, gleaming teeth.

Until finally, one twitched.

Gerhart was the first to charge, but Andreas was the first to draw blood.

FOUR

Lisi made haste delivering Gerwalta to the main farmhouse, a structure not insignificant in its size, and shared by several of the families that made the pack. The shewolf's muttered curses ended with, "A wolfsretter, on mine own hearth. The enemy at the gate, indeed," when she threw open the door of a wardrobe to sort through its contents.

Gerwalta tempered her instinct to argue. "I don't want to be the pack's enemy, Frau Kosner."

An acidic stare landed on her with scorching effects. "You became that when you let him bed you," Lisi spat. "What were you thinking, seducing a wolf? Don't you know that you've ruined him now? That he can never love another?"

"Neither can I." Never mind that the balance of the seducing had been on the wolf's side. Gerwalta caught a dash of white and pale yellow cloth that flew through the air. "Andreas is the man I love. The only man I'll ever love."

"Honeyed words, but you aren't a lupine. Your heart is fickle." Lisi turned to help the wolfsretter pull the frock down over her arms. "There, you are dressed. Now, if you'll forgive me, I need to see to our defense against certain death by your family. I advise you to stay here until someone comes for you. Andreas would hate if his blushing bride was harmed in the melee of battle, and I cannot guarantee your safety, Frau Baron."

Lisi left even as that term cracked open Gerwalta's heart. Frau Baron. True, Gerwalta had become Andreas's mate, but for some reason, in practical terms, that meant she now had a husband. In the eyes of all dark ones, Gerwalta was now Andreas's wife. Though why the wolves expected her to take on his name and not the other way around was a queer notion. She wasn't Frau Baron: he was Herr Faust.

And Herr Faust had another thing coming if he thought his wife was going to sit idly by while danger threatened. The wolves had a saying, 'mate before pack.' It was time for her to uphold her duty: defend her spouse from the greater threat, her clan. Above any wolf, Gerwalta knew the tactics and the weaknesses they evidenced, and by consequence, how best to defend against them. Surely, the pack wouldn't be so foolish as to turn away that kind of intelligence.

Right, then, time for war.

Gerwalta stepped down to the floor, gathered up her red cloak, and threw it over her shoulders. Let there be no confusion when her family arrived if she was among the enemy. She'd chosen her side, and it was with the wolves.

"You mustn't stand all in a group!" Gerwalta called out as she approached. "Wolfsretter raid tactics rely on the pack bunching together. You must spread out."

Lisi was the first to turn, the senior pack shewolf's eyes gaging wide.

"What is this now?" another of the women asked. "Think you can spread yourself for the king and then we'll all do the same? Go away, little red hood, or we're as liable to hurt you in the battle as the others."

Gerwalta ignored the remark and pressed on. "I have as much right to fight as you. My mate is my home, and you are his pack. I stand where my heart, not my blood, tells me."

The three other females exchanged looks before they began a slow pace in different directions. That was, until Lisi snapped at them.

"Where are you going?"

A shewolf with straw-colored hair and a blanched complexion fumbled. "The königinswolf ordered us to..."

Lisi's eyes squeezed shut. "She isn't queen-wolf, Esther. How could she be? She's not a wolf at all!"

16

Another of the females came to Esther's defense. "But she's Andreas's mate."

"And a wolfsretter!" Lisi rolled her eyes, clearly not understanding how her packmates could forget.

"You are right." Gerwalta turned. "I am no queen. I wouldn't assume any privilege as such. But I know Andreas loves each and every member of this pack. Please, I beg you, I know my family. For something like this, the hunting party will be small. Four warriors at most. Four on four are fair odds, but only if pitted evenly. Your lupine instinct to isolate one fight, four-on-one, isn't the best strategy."

Esther turned on Lisi. "Maybe she's right. When's the last time our pack was raided like this? None of us were alive then, I'm sure. If what Gerwalta says is true, then…"

"Now, now, is my wife's little sister spreading rumors."

The shewolf's words stopped as the rambling bass of a mighty male voice broke their ranks. The red-cloaked wolfsretter, chest plated with silver, carried a sword the height of half his body. A thick, burly black beard had grown so long, the ends of it had been braided. He held his weapon at the ready, and with a strong swing and good fortune, he was close enough for it to land among their throng.

The shewolves took their fur, an act which held both good and bad. Now Gerwalta couldn't directly communicate with them, but as wolves, they were more formidable foes.

"Coaching the mutts on defensive strategies?" he continued as he trod closer. "So it's true, then. You've forsaken your own to be another lupine bitch."

"Alexandre!" Gerwalta threw herself between the shewolves and Helga's husband. She cocked back an arm, ready to throw blows, though what her fist could do against a sword, who knew. Gerwalta reminded herself that she didn't have to hit Alexandre: she just had to throw him off balance and seize the silver. As a woman, it had stronger allegiance to her than him. "I don't want to hurt you, but I will if I need to."

Alexandre stopped where he was, grinning. "But the same isn't true for me. Besides, your mother only said we aren't to kill you.

She didn't say you needed to come back with all your limbs intact."

That Helga's spouse held the same contempt for Gerwalta as did his wife came as no surprise. No doubt Alexandre had also begrudged Gerwalta's ability to fly, a revelation which displaced the first-born daughter as heir apparent. He'd be delighted to do anything that corrected things, for certes. But why would Helga trust her husband to capture her? Surely her plotting sister would want to see through the deed herself.

Unless...

Why had a sole male been sent ahead and alone? Because he was a superior warrior? Hardly. To negotiate a truce? Wolfsretters didn't negotiate with wolves. There could be only one reason: because Helga was playing someone she thought a pawn, someone she wanted cleared from the game.

Poor Alexandre.

Alexandre spoke, bringing Gerwalta back to the moment. "Come quietly now, and I'll only kill one of these bitches. A man must have a little fun."

"According to my sister, you are a man who has quite a few little things."

A look of confusion glossed over the brute's face before wide eyes signaled clarity. "I satisfy my wife."

"Is that why she sent you here to die? Because she finds you so... satisfying?"

His face screwed up. "What are you talking about?"

"My sister is many vile things, but she isn't a fool. She would know you'd be no match for me," Gerwalta said. "Helga means for me to kill you, and while I'd not aid my sister's ambitions, I will protect my pack."

"Your pack?" Alexandre threw back his head and barked a laugh. "How rich! Fine then, little red shewolf, come get me if you think you can."

Gerwalta shifted as a flash of brown fur flew past. She barely had time to register the shewolf's movement before Alexandre was on his back, his sword a few feet away. She had less time still before the shewolf went flying back through the air, pushed away by her beastly brother-in-law. Lisi yelped as she crashed to the ground, but Gerwalta didn't turn. She couldn't let the distraction go to waste. The moment Alexandre's body surrendered, she lunged for the sword. By the time he turned on her again, Gerwalta was belly-down on the ground, eye-to-eye with her brother-in-law, the blade of the sword pressed to her palm. Later she'd tend the injury of its lick into her flesh, but the moment the metal heeded her command, the blade receded, forming a three-pronged dagger in its wake.

"You're a fourth daughter and a fifth child no one wanted. You wouldn't dare strike me down. Helga will—"

She waited no more. With a role, she was on her feet. Before Alexandre could manage to move his hulking mass the same way, the blow was delivered.

A crimson stream shot from Alexandre's chest in triplicate as the silver clawed in. Even as the life fled her brother-in-law's eyes, Gerwalta felt the metal twist and curl, his last attempt to reclaim its control. Too late and too little came of the effort. Within moments, the male wolfsretter went limp, his body kissing dust and snow.

Gerwalta gave herself a moment, then turned to the wolves. "The others will be upon us soon, and they won't make the same mistake of coming alone. Prepare. I'll attempt to find out more."

No time to waste. With a kick off the ground, she was airborne. Not too far off, the hunting party came into view. Three men, all of them her clan: her father, her brother Maximillian, and another of her brothers-in-law, Helmut. Coming up the rear, the mastermind herself, Helga.

There were still guests at the schloss from the wedding that had never happened; surely amongst them were any number of finely gifted hunters the Matron could've called upon. That the three approaching were males of her own clan confirmed what Alexandre had said. She was to be brought back alive. That gave the wolves a power they didn't know they had.

Gerwalta brought herself back to ground and turned to the

shewolves. "Three males, all of them of my clan. They have been ordered to capture me, but they will kill you if you get in the way. I shall not abandon you, but if one of you comes into imminent danger, you will give me up to save yourselves, is that understood? I escaped the schloss once, I can do it again."

Or at least, she hoped so.

FIVE

The farmhouse bell heralded the inevitable: wolfsretters were in the packlands, uninvited. Andreas fought past the instinct to abandon battle and run to the defense of the shewolves on the western ridge. He would need to trust in them to hold off the raid until Gerhart had gotten the better of him. Trust them, he lectured himself. Trust your Gerwalta.

His Gerwalta. Had he known when he'd risen with the moon that the night would end with her in his arms? And when the bond of their mating set in... He'd loved her before, but nothing compared to the intensity in the wake of their mating. Before, his heart smoldered. Now it blazed, a fire which fueled his every thought and gesture.

Gerhart's body slammed Andreas into the ground and back into the moment.

Lupine language in wolf form was not that of poetry. It communicated grand notions, overarching thoughts. Gerhart's growl was unmistakable in its meaning, however.

Surrender.

Andreas hadn't time to right himself before the wolf formerly of the Wehr pack was upon him, his teeth closing over the base of Andreas's throat. He reared up, his bottom half twisting to find purchase of the ground. Andreas almost righted himself when Gerhart pivoted and pulled, dragging him some distance before finally clenching his jaw.

No pain had ever been more welcome, for in it a king would be born. Andreas whined, a high-pitched sound meant to signal his surrender. Within moments, he felt it: the mystical ebb, the animalistic trophy that he'd claimed when he'd become königswolf just two years before. It fell away from him now, leaving him weakened but happy. Finally, for he didn't know how much longer he could withstand the

21

attack. Now, as soon as Gerhart released his hold and Andreas recalled his flesh, the new king could proclaim him exiled and remove the reason for the wolfsretter to attack the pack.

As soon as he let go...

Why wasn't he letting go?

"Gerhart..."

Pain turned to panic as Wilhelm's voice eked through Andreas's thoughts. Air... He couldn't get enough air.

"Gerhart!"

The axis of the world shifted as black fur streaked through the air. Andreas gasped, spinning over unto all fours, reclaiming his flesh. His hand flew to his throat. Puncture wounds, but luckily, over his collar bone, the highest alone in soft flesh. He'd heal in a week or two, if he kept the wound clean.

If he was still alive...

Andreas shot to his feet, turning to see what had happened. His eyes found the pair just in time: Gerhart crawling out from under Wilhelm's paw. Wilhelm had interfered, but did he wait long enough? Was Gerhart now king?

Both wolves took on their lay forms, as the younger pup spun on the pack's second.

"How dare you interfere!" Gerhart bellowed. "He was mine to destroy!"

"That wasn't the arrangement," Wilhelm snapped back. "You were to defeat him fairly in battle only. You took victory. You are now königswolf, we all feel it."

"And is it your role, Wilhelm, to decide my mind?" Gerhart's arm lashed out as he pointed an accusing finger at Andreas. "He brought the wrath of the wolfsretters upon us all, just so he could bed a whore."

Rage filled the fallen king. He drove forward, his ready to strike. "Call my mate a whore again and I'll wear your entrails as my skin."

Instead of take the bait, Gerhart put up a hand. "Stop!"

And he did. Not because he wanted it. Not because he willed it. But because Gerhart had commanded it. Because Gerhart was king.

Before Andreas had too long to ponder on the consequences of that truth, Wilhelm was between them.

"As second, it is my duty to bow to the king's demand, but it is my duty to call him out when one of his decisions is in his own interest instead of the pack's." Accusing eyes shifted to Andreas before they turned back. "The wolfsretters are coming and they'll want Andreas dead. But if you deny them their own justice, they'll take the punishment out on all of us. Exile him now, Gerhart, and let him carry their rage away in his wake."

Conflict warred across Gerhart's features. The king threaded his hair, tugging at the roots. Finally, after some hemming and hawing, he turned on Andreas. "You must never return."

Andreas nodded. "Now do it, Gerhart. I'll thank you for it."

"You'll thank me?" Gerhart laughed. "I'm not saving your life today, Andreas. I merely forestall your death. Without a pack, you'll slowly go insane. The wolfsretter will have your blood then, there is nothing to stop that."

It was a truth Andreas couldn't argue, but he had to have faith that he and Gerwalta would find a pack willing to take them in. First, however, this one must be saved.

"Wilhelm," Gerhart said, turning to the second. "Go immediately to the front line; meet the wolfsretters and tell them I am king and that Andreas Baron is no longer a member of this pack."

Wilhelm snapped straight as a board. "Yes, mein könig." Which upon, he made to leave.

"Oh, before you go, Wilhelm?"

The second turned.

A sinister smile waxed over the king's face. "If they refuse to accept this as grounds to withdraw, give the order to the shewolves and a howl to arms: kill all on sight, starting with Andreas's unholy mate."

"What? No, you cannot—"

Andreas doubled over as Gerhart's fist connected with his gut. "You have your wish, Andreas. You are hereby exiled."

All the air rushed from Andreas's lungs as the magic was made so, and he was left alone, wild to the world.

SIX

It wasn't two flicks of a lamb's tail before the other wolves took their fur and followed in Wilhelm's wake. Gerhart waited to be last, allowing himself one more menacing glare at the fallen king before his flesh rippled and his maw grew long.

Alone, it came down upon Andreas: the emptiness, the utter sense that he was alone in the world. Packless. Exiled. It was what he'd asked for, but he couldn't have anticipated how it overwhelmed. Discouragement melted into his marrow, a sense that he'd taken the first step toward his own doom. And very well, he might have. But then, the lupine turned on himself, lecturing.

"Gerwalta still needs you," he said, leaving unspoken even if the pack does not.

The pack. He could do nothing for them now but leave and hope the Matron quickly squashed Gerhart's rebellion without casualty.

The blood on his chest had already begun to dry, the puncture wounds won in battle ebbing in their intensity. Taking his fur again risked exasperating their severity, however, as the shift from man to beast would reshape his body. He had to get to Gerwalta and he had to do it on two feet. Resolve infused his spine. Andreas turned, prayed, and ran.

Fur and red cloaks marked the sparring warriors from each side just beyond the farmhouse. Andreas narrowed his eyes, trying to discern which side held advantage and learn where his beloved stood. Desperate eyes raked the ground, searching. Dizziness crushed him as he tried to advance, sending Andreas to his knees just as he heard someone call out his name. He turned his eyes to the sky just as Gerwalta lowered into view.

A frown flitted across her face as she laid hands on him, feeling out his wounds. "You're injured."

He nodded with some difficulty as he captured her hands with his own. "Gerhart defeated me fairly, though he also tried to kill me. It will heal."

Given that Gerwalta's expression didn't shift, Andreas guessed this came as no surprise to her. "He lunged for me the moment he was in sight, but Helga and the men of my clan arrived just in time to draw him off. Helga and he are squaring off now, I suppose. I hope with words and not violence."

"He's a fool if he challenges your sister."

"He's a brave and bold king," Gerwalta said. "Helga wasn't given leave to kill anyone else in the pack or she'd have done it without coming into view. She saw me leave; as soon as her line pushed through the pack, they will follow the direction I flew. Are you safe to move? We must make haste."

"I cannot take my fur without reopening my wounds. I'll have to go on two feet, but I think if I... Gerwalta!"

She hadn't waited for him to finish his thoughts. Instead, Gerwalta hooked the lupine under the arms and lifted off. Soon, his feet skimmed the tops of the trees as she whisked them over the valley. For the first time, Andreas truly grasped why a wolfsretter who could fly was such a threat. He was terrified out of his good senses. Surely, she recalled that lupines feared heights?

"Forest... High... Air... Fall..."

"I would never drop you, love, but I cannot go far like this," was her reply to his ramblings. "Do you have a cache of clothing somewhere?"

Gerwalta changed course just as the sun kissed the horizon. The crimson fingers of dawn reached out and stung his eyes. He pointed toward the waterfall that rose above the village, too terrified to speak.

She bobbed her head. "Good, because it is morning and laymen tend to notice flying women carrying naked men about."

They took the laymen's roads. If Helga's hunting party managed to catch up, apprehending them would be more difficult with witnesses.

"We have to figure out where to go."

Andreas's words broke her from her thoughts. Gerwalta kept her pace strong as she could without looking like she was running away. "I already know where we're going: Navarre. Karahan is going to pay me back what he owes me by giving us sanctuary."

She jerked back as Andreas took her hand and pulled. "I've a little more than two months," he said. "Two months to find a pack that won't only accept me but will also accept a wolfsretter as a mate. We cannot spend it hiding out with vampires."

"You'll only be able to go mad if we are still alive. Until we get out of any area my mother holds influence if not control over, no pack will be safe. Navarre isn't ideal, but it's ruled by the Casa de Amarillo and they detest the House of Red. A pack under their guard is far more likely to be accepting of..."

"The packs of Iberia are itinerant, religious zealots!" Andreas said, cutting her off. "Insofar as either of us heed the church, we are both Protestant. They may not kill us for our mating, but they'll never offer us a place in their realm."

She ground her teeth until it sent pain shooting into her temple. "Where else would we even have a hope? Unless you want to try for the Americas, in which case we'll need to figure out how to conceal your lupine condition during the... What is it, two months it takes to get there? You are no longer a königswolf, Andreas. You won't be able to keep your laity form during the full moon."

Anger infused his tone with gruff. "Do you not think that I'm aware that I'm no longer king? I've sacrificed my pack and my position for us, Gerwalta. I know that in your customs women rule, but can you add that to my balance and for once, just let me decide our course?"

Her face grew taut with rage. "This isn't about me being a woman, this is about strategic thinking! We can flee to neither wolf nor wolfsretter—not immediately, anyhow. We need an impartial and powerful ally before we approach anyone. And sacrifice? Do you think I've made no sacrifice?" Her arm lashed back in the direction of the village. "I just killed one of my own clan to save members of your pack. Now, my sentence is the same as yours: death. Merciless, unconditional death."

Her admission managed to still his tongue. Andreas took a step back. "I'm sorry, I didn't know."

His apology also softened her resolve. Gerwalta crossed her arms over her stomach. "It was a thing required."

"Even, still…" Andreas drew a deep inhale and pushed the air out through pursed lips, even as the gesture tickled the pain. "Gerwalta, love, I understand what you are saying, but I think it best to try for England. If we can find Stephen's pack, they would take us in to settle the life debt if nothing else."

"But England is no small country, Andreas. Do you have any idea where precisely he might be?"

Andreas's chin dropped into his chest. "I've had no word from my brother since parting ways in Nuremberg. But please, Walta," he looked up, the biggest set of puppy eyes she had ever seen set in his face, "consider my reasons, and that there is truth in what I say."

She turned then, refusing to be manipulated by emotions— his or hers. In the wider scope of consequences, she couldn't deny that Andreas's plan held advantages. Stephen and his pack formed of stolen seconds from across the Holy Roman Empire wouldn't be alive if not for their mercy. How could they be turned away? But Gerwalta also knew that the Isles were the Verdant Realm, overseen by the House of Green. The Reds were infamous for their strict character, but the Greens were renowned for their incorporation into the politics of the laymen around them. They could travel no easier through cities there than they could through the forests, and that would be if they knew where to go when they landed in some English port.

"Perhaps," she admitted finally. "But at least with Navarre, we know our destination. What if we were to go there first and ask Karahan to use his contacts to find Stephen's pack for us? Vampires can travel thrice as fast if properly motivated."

"And what would we motivate them with? We haven't any coin of any realm."

"If I can get my hands on more silver, I can create any realm's coin. Grand churches often have plenty."

The rigidity of his features softened, though Andreas refused to yield. She drew a deep breath as she realized she must take her own advice. She was mated to a wolf, and among their kind, it was the male who made decisions. She would need to submit to Andreas on some things on occasion.

Even if he were wrong.

"I've made my best argument and yield to your counsel. What say you?"

Hands on his hips, Andreas chewed on his thoughts. "To Navarre. For a start." He grimaced. "Well, that wasn't so bad."

Confusion drew her eyebrows down. "What wasn't?"

"Our first mated row." The lupine closed the distance between them, his hands settling on her hips and his lips, to hers. The kiss was gentle, tentative. "And our first reconciliation. I've heard rumors that such events are made more grounded by an act of the flesh..."

Heat swept through her body. "Perhaps when we've put more ground behind us."

He nodded as he again brushed a kiss. "Let us go then, and put, as you say, 'some ground behind us,' so that later, I can put some ground beneath us instead."

Her knees threatened to revolt, but Gerwalta lectured her body into submission. She nearly changed her mind when, turning to continue up the road, his palm flattened against her backside.

She had thought their lovemaking may be unbalanced, both as the dominant sex of their kind and thus, out of harmony. Reality was proving a keen teacher, however. They would both demand dominance in the marital bed, and by such measure, both come out on top.

In all the glorious ways possible.

SEVEN

A crimson staff of twilight sunset fell across her closed eyes, bringing Gerwalta Faust back to the world of the living. A heavy weight across her hips and a warm body behind her brought a smile. Waking up beside one's beloved truly was a delight. More delightful still when one's beloved proved an amorous beast once... aroused.

Though it was not without consequence. Her hips were sore. Her lips, swollen. The grass stains present on both palms and knees would probably endure for some time. Yes, they'd both lost a good deal to be together, but certain things they'd gained counterbalanced their sacrifices.

Truth be told, it may actually be a gain.

Andreas would continue to slumber under the last rays of light unless she woke him. As tempting as it may be, she knew he needed rest. His recovery from the injury he'd sustained amazed her; she didn't think a wolf unmoored from a pack could achieve such progress in a week. The flesh wounds had vanished, leaving only marred skin and bruises. Whatever miracle had caused it, she'd not demand payment for blessings. Andreas, on the other hand, reveled in it. Each day, he seemed to grow less somber and more... well, drunk on her love. It was almost like he had a secret he was concealing, some wonderful surprise he'd spring on her to blow her away.

But what could that possibly be? They'd both escaped the Schwarzwald with their lives and not much more. If he'd managed to find out some gift for her, he had grifted in from laymen in one of the villages they passed. They both agreed they needed the silver to trade, but that they wouldn't take more than necessary. She didn't therefore think it likely he'd stolen just to flatter her.

Gerwalta rose, pulling on the laity clothes they'd stolen from a drying line a few days back, and worked the silver she'd siphoned from a church in Friedberg back over her arm. Its gentle embrace renewed her. Of course, sleeping in Andreas's arms did have some cost: her silver must be shoved off lest it burn him in intimate moments. Now with it back on her person, she strode off into the forest, hoping to find some woodland creature to make their evening meal.

Not a quarter of an hour into her quest, scattered amongst mighty pines, deer grazed. A young buck died with haste and mercy. Of course, they couldn't consume the whole thing between the two of them, but Gerwalta refused to take one of the smaller does. It was early spring now, the time of nature's renewal. Likely many of the females were with child, and hungry though she was, what kind of hunter would strike down pregnant prey?

Gerwalta let her legs collapse beneath her as she withdrew the silver-made-spear from the spent creature's chest and made of it a blade to clean what they needed from it, when a familiar voice floated down from above.

"You don't eat it raw, do you?"

The deer was forgotten as she turned the blade skyward. Gunda Faust descended with utter care, meticulously lowering herself until her feet impressed upon the dewy, newly sprung grass, and continued.

"I ask," her mother said, "because I wonder how many of our traditions you've forsaken already. Tell me, do you cook the meat, or have you taken to pulling it bloody from the bone as does your lupine mate?"

Gerwalta weighed her options. She could run, but even she didn't think herself capable of besting her mother's speed. Even flying she would be at the mercy of pulling Andreas's weight. She might be able to land her blade in her mother's chest, but the chances that Gunda wasn't wearing her own silver plated beneath her tunic were slim. Her only solution, therefore, was to play out the scene and hope a solution or advantage emerged.

"We need not give up ourselves to become each other's," she said, keeping the blade between them nonetheless. "I cook it; he eats it raw, but I doubt you've tracked us so far and so long to ask culinary questions. What is it you want from us, Mother?"

"Your obeisance." Gunda's grin flattened. "Andreas Barron will return with me to Triberg. Whether that is in chains or in pieces depends on you."

"Andreas has no cause to return to Triberg. He is no longer king. He was fairly defeated in battle and exiled; no one in the Schwarzwald has any claim to him."

One of Gunda's eyebrows quirked. "And you do?"

"I am his mate. I am the only one whose claim matters."

Gunda blew out an exhale through pursed lips, her eyes turned to the ground. "Why are you intent on making this so difficult? This wolf has lain with you and his heart can never be turned, but that doesn't mean you need share his fate."

"You never were particularly keen on the non-political and emotional aspects of marriage, were you? No, you weren't. Then how could you possibly understand that my heart is just as bound as his?"

"This is youth and romanticism talking, both of which fade with time." When again Gunda raised her eyes, it was with such tenderness in her gaze that it forced Gerwalta to take a step back. "Only honor survives the grave. Only family and power preserve you from it. Please, daughter, I would have you live, even if in exile. I wouldn't wear my own blood on my hands."

The tiny part of her that had always preened itself for her mother's acceptance and approval nearly took control, but Gerwalta shoved it down. "You would have me return when we both know I slew Alexandre? Even if you managed to somehow twist the truth and pin the death on the wolves, which, knowing your tactics, you've no doubt already conceived, do you think your first-born daughter will let your fourth-born live?"

"I don't even know if she'll let me live."

Another mental blow which challenged Gerwalta's balance. "What do you mean?"

"You brought an asp into our home. Mehmet is twice the snake Helga is, and they brood in their shared mayhem," the Matron explained. "I beg you, forfeit Andreas's life and let me save you, because someday soon, you may need to save me."

Gerwalta's hand flew over her face, as though a foul smell had crept into the air. "Chasing me down, then... It's not about recovering me. It's not even about punishing Andreas. Both are just mechanisms to save yourself."

"If I'm not successful in returning you both to court, mark my words, Helga will come, and what mercy I am willing to show will render me a saint in comparison."

"I don't need saints, and I don't need you." The younger wolfsretter turned to leave, now confident that a dagger wouldn't land in her back when she did. "Follow us no more."

Gerwalta had only managed two steps when it happened.

Silver rope encircled her ankles. She fell, flipped, tried to command the metal to yield, but it would not. It stayed, immovable. In moments, another lash of silver twisted itself around her wrists, trussing her like an animal to be taken to market.

Or a wolfsretter to be taken as prisoner.

"There's no use struggling." Gerwalta looked up from the ground upon which she lay to see her mother, the end of the cording wrapped around her hand, stalking toward her. "This is blood-claimed silver. It heeds only my command."

But the silver Gerwalta wore under her clothing had no such limitations. No sooner had she bid it, however, then she felt it siphon off her, running down the cord that bound her to her mother.

"Did you really think you could rebuff me with your own supply? I am a matron; you are an insolent child. Your will can never best mine."

"And yet, I had the will to follow my heart instead of your command, didn't I?" Gerwalta flexed, writhed, pulled, all in a futile effort to free herself. "Let me go before..."

But it was too late. A swish of leaves, a snap of twig, and a mat of fur flew from the foliage.

Gunda let go her hold, but it was only to form a blade intended for the werewolf flying straight for her.

EIGHT

He reached out for her the moment he knew himself awake but found her not.

One eyelid cracked open to confirm that what his hand had found was true; Gerwalta wasn't where she had been when they'd fallen asleep at dawn. Mayhap she'd ventured off to hunt? It was a wolf's duty to provide but such was a wolfsretter. Not that he begrudged the game she'd managed to capture. Gerwalta was a gifted huntress, and Andreas, a lupine of tremendous appetite.

He stretched out long, his limbs going up then akimbo, before the former king turned on his side and folded back in on himself. The breeze blew across his face, bringing him insight into a shift in the weather. So far, they'd been fortunate to encounter agreeable conditions. It had rained one day, but only lightly. Now the air smelled of heat and moisture and a tingle of unresolved winds. There would be lightning soon, and he'd need to get Gerwalta somewhere safe until it passed.

"Gerwalta?" Andreas called out, his eyes closing against the wane of slumber. "Love, there's a tempest brewing. Are you near? We'll need to leave soon."

His ears sorted through the sounds of the forest, of the stir of deer catching the last bit of grass before bedding down. Of the owl flapping its wings in a nearby tree, it too shaking off the last vestiges of sleep. Of the mouse already scurrying. Of the...

Andreas shot to his feet and pulled in a series of rapid, short breaths, turning in a slow arc. Three-quarters through his rotation, understanding came to him. The lupine didn't dwell to consider strategy or consequence. His mate was in peril, and if his senses could be believed, it was because their escape hadn't been as successful as they hoped.

He jumped, took his fur, and landed on padded paws, eating

up the forest floor. Andreas's heart raced. His fear upset the balance of man and beast within. If Gerwalta was unharmed, he would fight to free her. If she was injured or worse, then the cloak of the Matron wouldn't be the only red to spill across the forest today.

It seemed to take forever for him to reach the clearing. Gerwalta lay on the ground, both her wrists and her ankles bound. As the profile of the scents processed, the aroma of blood was undeniable. She moved, so she still lived. Thank God, then he need only free her. The silver cords which ran from his beloved to her maniacal mother's grasp would burn like hell when he hit them, but if he was lucky, he'd knock them hard enough to loosen the Matron's grip.

He didn't see the blade until he was already sailing through the air.

"Andreas, no!"

His beloved's words cleaved his soul. No, he couldn't leave her. He couldn't let her go on alone. They'd suffered too much, given up too much to be together, for it all to end so soon. All this occurred to him in the flash of a moment, but what could he do? A second or two more, and he'd fall upon the Matron's blade. Gunda Faust was a seasoned warrior, an expert huntress. She knew precisely where to hold her weapon so that it would strike deep into his heart when he landed upon it. And in that moment of accepting his fate, of recognizing he was powerless to change it, Andreas understood how to survive.

The Matron meant to strike down a wolf.

But if a man fell upon the blade instead, her position was all wrong.

Andreas forced his body through the quickest transformation he'd ever experienced and paid the cost. His nerves sizzled, his head pounded, his muscles contorted and spasmed. The lupine didn't know where the pain he'd pushed himself through ended and where that caused by the Matron's weapon began, but he did know this... He wasn't dead.

Given the torment he now experienced, perhaps this was the worse fate.

"Mother, no!"

His arrival must have created a circumstance that allowed Gerwalta to break free from her bonds. Soon, her body covered his, bringing Andreas back to his purpose. He did this to save her, to protect her, to protect his family.

Only when his mate wrapped her hands around the hilt of the dagger buried in his shoulder and yanked it from its corporeal bedding did he understand where he'd been struck. A shoulder... Good. That would heal. But given that the injury was silver-born, it would take some time.

If they survived this, their journey just became all that more difficult.

"Move and I'll finish the beast off, put him out of his mercy."

It was the Matron who spoke, but her words had the opposite effect. Gerwalta laid herself over his writhing body, bringing to Andreas's mind a fresh litany of fears. He had to quell the pain, bring himself under control. If his flailing did her damage, he'd never forgive himself.

"Kill us both or let us be," Gerwalta declared, "but I'll not yield."

"Mercy!" His own words sounded like those of another, his voice hollowed by pain, even as his shaking began to subside. "Matron, mercy for her."

"I am attempting to be merciful!" Gunda snapped. "A month spent in the dungeon, a flogging before the court, but she'll live."

Hot tears streamed from the corner of his eyes as Andreas shook his head. "No, not just for Gerwalta," he said. "For... For our child."

A chill settled over Andreas's body as Gerwalta shot to her feet. "What?"

Andreas looked up, seeing the faint embers of twilight's fade dance across her face. "You are with child. Three or four days now, but still."

Gerwalta's hand slid down over her midsection. "I'm... Oh, Andreas!"

But as his mate fell to her knees and threw her arms around his body, difficult given his inclined position, the Matron reminded them that her task was left undone, and she demanded satisfaction.

"Impossible!" she hissed out through clenched teeth. "You only consummated a week ago. There is no way for it to … How could you possibly know?"

With Gerwalta's aid, Andreas pushed himself up, using the side uninjured in the attack. In moments, she had conjured her cloak and pulled it off, using it as a compress for the wound. "I am a lupine; I noticed the change in her scent."

Gunda remained incredulous. "Something which you've concealed from her only to conveniently blurt out when I've arrived to remedy your crimes?"

"I've been waiting to tell her. I didn't think that Gerwalta should carry the burden of knowing until she was safe."

Gunda's silver siphoned back under her sleeves as she bit her bottom lip. "A child… It cannot be. What fate would it have? Half lupine, half wolfsretter? Our laws forbid this. Neither fold would claim it."

"It wouldn't matter if she were to be half suckling pig, Mother, we will claim it," Gerwalta said. "Hate me if you must, wish me ill, but our child has committed no wrong. Will you condemn it too? Will you condemn me along with her?"

Gerwalta had never known her mother to be the kind who shuddered, but that didn't change truth. Gunda Faust veritably vibrated, the fingers of her weapon hand flexing, opening, flexing, opening. Vexed, she paced the forest floor.

"Mother?" Gerwalta took a hesitant step forward. "Mother, please. Do not destroy your grandchild and kill an innocent child merely for the fact that its parents erred in your eyes."

Gunda's gaze flew up, even as her chin remained tucked into her chest. "A lupine is never innocent."

"But a wolfsretter is." Gerwalta motioned behind her back, asking for leniency in her remarks from her husband. "Our child is as much of your bloodline as it is Andreas's. Would you destroy a wolfsretter thus?"

The salve of tenderness applied, Gerwalta waited, unmoving, frozen in her pose, for the sentiments to sink into her mother's skin. After a few moments, it came: the change, the resolution, the shift.

"I would not." Gunda lifted her head. "But your sister would."

Gerwalta nodded solemnly. "Is she with you on this hunt?"

"If she were, you'd already be dead."

A stark truth, but the truth nonetheless. Gerwalta licked her lips. "Tell her I died, mother. Tell her you killed us both and burned the bones, your rage so hot it wouldn't allow patience enough to return us."

"She'll never believe that I let go a chance to humiliate you both. I need... I need proof."

Andreas asked, "What would it take to convince her?"

"Nothing short of a body." The Matron's eyes focused on the wolf's leg. "Or perhaps she'd concede with only part of one."

In a flash, Gerwalta covered Andreas. "No. No, absolutely not. He couldn't possibly—"

"I'll do it."

Gerwalta shot a dagger's stare at her mate. "You will not."

"I will too, Walta." Andreas hobbled in the Matron's direction, past his wife too stunned by the act to attempt to pull him back. Raising both hands, the left still shaking, he looked at them in turn before dropping his right side. "This paw does less for me."

Gerwalta attempted to part them. "Mother, don't you dare. This is too high a price. Too high!"

"If it buys us our freedom and our pup's life..." The lupine stepped in closer, around his mate. "Take it, Matron. Fair payment: my paw for her heart." He nodded in Gerwalta's direction. "Though the favor of balance would still lay with me."

The Matron eyeballed the offering, her lips tight as she peered at something it seemed she didn't quite believe. Gunda summoned silver, shaping in her hands a blade in the shape of the crescent moon and as long as her forearm. She passed one more look up to her daughter. "You concur?"

Gerwalta's wet eyes belied her resolute exterior. "I do."

Gunda took Andreas's hand in hers as she pivoted, giving her the proper angle from which to strike. "The blade would cut cleaner through a narrower juncture. Perhaps if you took your wolf, Andreas. Yes, that would do better. Take your fur, and I'll take your paw, and in doing so, give you both your freedom."

The birds of the forest, only just settled in for the night, fled their nocturnal harbor and took to the sky.

NINE

Karahan jumped from the table the moment Gerwalta's form slipped into view. "Lady Baron, you are positively glowing this evening."

Andreas took a step back, allowing their host to dote upon his wife. At first, the werewolf had questioned the vampire's fervent attentions, but had simply come to recognize in the five miraculous months in which they'd been guests of Lord of the Dracule that Karahan was, at heart, a family man. That held even if he'd recently employed Gerwalta's services to trap most of his.

"But now, you are flushed," the vampire continued as he guided Gerwalta toward the table. "Are you feeling well?"

The blush that blew across Gerwalta's cheeks when she met his eyes matched Andreas's own. "Oh, quite well."

Karahan followed her gaze, and upon seeing the smirk on Andreas's face, cleared his throat as he lowered her into her chair, Gerwalta supporting the swell of her stomach with her own hand.

"Master Baron, any further pain?"

Andreas held up the absence of his hand in response to Karahan's question. Where once there had been a paw, now only a scarred stump remained. In the end, it had bought them their freedom, and what more can he ask than that? Still, how would he love to have had run his fingers through Gerwalta's long, auburn hair one more time.

"Every day, it aches less," the lupine said. "Thank you for your concern."

He nodded, turning back to his cup of tea. Another thing he'd learned of vampires. Yes, they required blood to maintain life, but they were also great fans of drinking any liquid in general and did so at grant lengths recreationally. This he observed again as they sat for their evening meal; a dish of stewed rabbit which Andreas gulped down joyously, even if he did think the game was somewhat overcooked. And by overcooked, he meant cooked. Better for Gerwalta, he supposed, and beggars couldn't be choosers, could they? After some conversing and recounting the news among the laity of the day—apparently there had been some upset in the French court regarding their finance minister—Gerwalta and Andreas exchanged a look, nodding to each other that the moment had come.

"Lord Dracule," Gerwalta began.

"Please, Lady Baron, do call me Igor."

She grinned despite the interruption. "Very well, Igor. Andreas and I wanted again to offer our greatest thanks for your generosity since we arrived. If not for your kindness, we aren't certain where we could've gone."

Igor raised his glass in salute. "A debt was owed, one I've repaid with joy. Your company has been very welcomed in this land with sparse amusements."

"Be that as it may, your hospitality has far exceeded repayment. You've treated us as honored guests, catered not only to our needs, but many of our wants as well. It is something for which we'll be eternally grateful."

The smile faded from Igor's face. "I sense a pivot forthcoming."

Here, a hesitant Andreas took up. "Shortly after we arrived, I hired an emissary to seek my brother in England, to inquire if he would have us. Early this morning, word arrived that that emissary not only located Stephen in the north of that country, but that my mate and I would be welcome to join their pack."

"Join their pack?" Igor repeated the words as though their echo would bring clarity. "I'm sorry, I'm afraid I don't understand, where has my hospitality failed that you feel driven away?"

Gerwalta turned to Igor, crestfallen. "Our decision is in retaliation to nothing. We think merely of the welfare of the babe. A wolf needs a pack."

"And yet... here Andreas is, without one." Igor brought up an uncertain gaze to Andreas. "Please understand that what I'm about to say is only born out of my concern for you both. For you all. Given Gerwalta's condition and your incapacitation, you cannot think it wise to travel such a great distance."

Gerwalta wrapped her hand around her mate's, squeezing it as though she might squeeze the words from his tongue. "The fact that I am so far along is precisely the reason we feel it wise to go soon. Andreas has avoided the lunacity that customarily claims exiled wolves by virtue of our child. The magic that binds a pack has bonded him and our babe to save them both, but who knows if it'll endure after the birth, or if the same will be true of our child."

"And from a practical position," Andreas added, "even among dark ones, not all births are successful. If, Lord forbid, there should be a complication with the delivery…"

His words tapered off, but Gerwalta was a wolfsretter, a creature born of rougher materials than those from which sentiment were fashioned. "If the baby doesn't survive, we don't know how long the effects of lunacity can be avoided," she added. "And if I do not survive, at least I'll go to my grave knowing that Andreas and Brünhild have a pack and family to keep them safe."

"I told you, love, I don't care for that name," Andreas cooed. "Besides, we do not know if it is a girl."

"It is a girl," Gerwalta persisted.

"If that is your wish, then." Igor stood and buttoned his jacket. "I'll have the servants ready what supplies they can and arrange for trusted men with proper knowledge to escort you to England and see that you are settled there properly."

Andreas rose to his feet in kind. "That is very kind, but we must make our way alone."

The vampire guffawed. "I don't understand why you would refuse so generous an offer, and from such a prestigious member of the dark one community. Many would be honored."

Andreas bowed, his disfigured arm resting against his abdomen. "Indeed, we are honored, but both Gerwalta and I are aware that our safety depends upon our ability to be covert. A werewolf and a wolfsretter, the latter visibly expecting, traveling in comfort with the aid of a prominent vampire's retinue would attract attention. The more hands that reach out to assist us lead to more tongues that might disclose our existence."

Igor took the explanation in full before nodding. "Then I will accompany you personally."

Gerwalta clicked her tongue. "You don't mean to leave your own daughter behind in Navarre alone, do you? Igor, you yourself said that Inga's penance is being served only by virtue of your regular visits at the monastery at which you've left her."

The vampire planted balled fists on his hips and sighed into his chest. "Then at least accept my best wishes and prayers for your safe journey?"

Gerwalta grinned. "I would never refuse that. Please know that I'll always look back at the months we were here as some of the happiest in my life. Your debt, sir, is paid in full."

"No, Frau Baron, I fear it is not."

TEN

Someone touched her, and it wasn't someone she knew.

The moment Gerwalta's eyes flew open, she jolted up, ready to dismember whoever had the audacity to push his fingertips into her person. The woman was of small carriage, with olive skin and a gaunt face that went white at the sight of her. Gerwalta's senses reached out for silver but were left wanting. None was near. Only as rationality rose up within her did she recall that no silver was kept in the chamber she shared with her lupine husband.

The husband who, in fact, had just placed himself between her and the stranger dressed in red.

Was it her clan? Had they come for them? Her eyes went wide, her heart raced.

"Gerwalta, it's only the midwife. Be calm."

Her spirits ebbed as she gained perspective. Yes, there was a stranger, but the woman was of the laity. Both Igor and Andreas stood near; if this newcomer meant her harm, either would have her throat out in moments. Midwife? Had they lost their...

"The baby?" Gerwalta pushed herself up in the bed, her back against the wooden headboard as she ran hands over her abdomen.

Andreas prostrated himself at her side, reaching up to pet her hair with his remaining hand. "The babe is well. But you swooned, and we wanted to be certain you were too."

Swooned? What kind of wolfsretter swooned? But then again, as she searched her memory, she couldn't recall what had led to this moment. She'd been walking back in from the gardens when she scented something burning upon the air. That drew her to one of the hearths in the castle; if the laity staff were in danger from some breakout of fire, she wished to help. Then suddenly, smoke, as thick as it was black, blinded her.

She must have been overcome.

"And Igor?"

Gerwalta passed a look to the man she normally welcomed in her presence. But the moment seemed much too intimate for the oversight of a vampire.

Andreas shrugged. "He insisted no one he was unfamiliar with personally was to be anywhere near you." The werewolf leaned in. "And you think I'm overprotective."

"You would be as overly protective if you had my centuries of experience in court politics," the vampire mumbled. "And it is rude to speak of someone present in third person."

"It was not our intention to snub, Igor."

Igor was unimpressed by good humor. Any further discussion on the matter, however, was interrupted when the midwife said something in that peculiar mix of tongues the locals spoke. The vampire was kind enough to translate.

"As best she can tell, both mother and child are fine," the vampire reported. "But she wishes to hear the same from Gerwalta's own lips."

If the baby was well, she'd soldier through anything. But there was something upsetting her. Something that needed addressing. "I am... I am monstrously hungry."

Andreas and Igor cracked smiles, as did the midwife when Igor made the words plain to her. The small woman bowed and left.

"She's going to stop by the kitchens on the way down," Igor said. "They'll send something up directly."

Andreas sat at the edge of the bed, taking her hands to his lips. "Walta, love, what happened?"

She tried her memory. "I'm not certain. I smelled smoke, I followed..."

46

"Smoke?" Andreas turned to Igor. "Has there been any fire reported by your staff?"

"None, and surely a wolf could detect it on the air better than could I."

"How bizarre..." Gerwalta searched her thoughts for some better clue until her groaning stomach stole back her attention. "Andreas, I really am quite famished. Are there no victuals at the ready?"

He laughed. "Soon, love. Marta only now just... Walta? Walta, where are you going?"

At least he was wise enough not to attempt to coax her back into bed. Andreas had learned early in their pairing the pointlessness of arguing Gerwalta out of her decisions. So, when she swept past him and out into the hall, the only thing the lupine could do was follow, as did the vampire, though out of concern or merely for the entertainment, she knew not.

It wasn't as much her thought as her nose that led her out of their suite, down the stairs, through the small hall where oft they dined, and into the part of the castle used by the servants. The scent of laundering intensified, as did a handful of others that didn't interest her. On, on and on Gerwalta went, seeking out the aroma that tickled her senses and made her mouth water.

The moment she entered the kitchens, she saw it. Manna. Lorded over by one, single servant. The bald layman looked up when she came to a standstill before the carcass he'd been butchering. He spoke no German—no one except Igor and Andreas did—but he had originated from a region north of Navarre and Gerwalta had discovered a fortnight before he spoke French.

"Madame?" He asked, dropping his cleaning knife on the table and giving her his full attention.

Gerwalta swallowed back the saliva building in her mouth. "What animal is this, Antoine?"

He glanced over the skinless, headless, footless thing between them. "Ox, madame. Freshly slaughtered not an hour ago. Cook was thinking to use it to—"

She heard no more as the sound of her own pulse sped. Gerwalta attacked face-first. The moment her teeth hit bone and blood filled her mouth, she felt it: relief. This, yes, this was all she had wanted. With another bit, she filled her mouth and found her heaven.

"Walta, love?" Andreas's hands settled on her shoulder. "Are you—"

She couldn't explain from where the feral growl that left her mouth had come, nor could she have made such a noise on command. The only thing she knew was that another wolf was near, and she had no intention of sharing.

Her mouth went slack in the echo of her own thoughts. Another wolf?

Gerwalta's hand flew to her mouth as she fell back. "Good lord, what am I doing?"

Igor, his step tenuous to avoid the early morning sun coming in through a nearby doorway, expressed the same query.

Andreas, however, was not as stumped. "You're craving fresh kill. It's very common among expecting shewolves."

"But I'm not a shewolf." Gerwalta stated the obvious. "I'm not a... Oh, Andreas, what is happening to me?"

Igor balanced his chin on his balled-up fist. "Remarkable. I'd always had the theory, but to see it in practice... Simply exceptional."

The wolfsretter pulled out of her husband's hold. "What, Igor? Do you know what's happening to me?"

"Well, to make it plain, you are carrying a wolf. Or at least, something that's wolf enough to make lupine demands of your palate. Antoine," Igor directed his words to the butcher, "I wonder if we might beg for a smaller knife Frau Baron could use? She may have a wolf's appetite, but she lacks one's teeth."

"I'm fine." Her next words muffled as her lips wrapped around the creature's hindquarter. Only when she nearly injured herself ripping off a morsel did she acquiesce and reach for the little angled blade the butcher had procured for her. No sooner had she touched it than she felt it... the sear of pain, the jolt of lightning made solid.

Gerwalta called out and dropped the blade, even as Igor with his vampiric speed caught it before it hit the ground.

"It... burns!" she gasped, dropping it in an instant.

Andreas was on Antoine in a moment. "How dare you?"

Only, the poor man, speaking not a lick of German, understood only two things. The pregnant woman's husband was angry, and he was also a werewolf who'd just sprouted very lupine fangs in a very red face.

"Unhand my servant, Andreas." The vampire remained completely calm. "Antoine did nothing but hand your wife a blade."

Andreas took a step back, though his heaving chest demonstrated his continued disquiet. "You saw how Gerwalta reacted. He must have done something to—"

White as a sheet, Gerwalta interrupted. "Antoine did nothing. The blade is silver, and silver burns wolves. Silver burned me. Am I—?" Her trembling arms crossed over her stomach as she turned and fled, the knife falling to the floor. She didn't wait to see if Andreas pursued her but hoped not. Should he ask her what was wrong, she knew her words would dig a dagger into his heart as much as if she had stabbed him herself.

ELEVEN

When the wind shifted, Gerwalta scented the vampire on the wind.

"I hope you don't take offense, Igor, when I tell you that I wish to be alone."

The vampire leaned against the wall beside her, just out of reach of the sunlight coming in through the open window. "I hope you don't take offense that I intend to ignore your request."

Planting her hands, she pushed herself back a bit, landing her in a less precarious position. "I assure you, I am well. Or will be, if given a little space."

"Are you certain? You are, after all, sitting on a window ledge four stories off the ground."

"You forget, I can fly."

"To fly is a choice. You could equally choose to fall. In fact, I don't doubt the thought has crossed your mind. Oh, not the intention, though few in your situation would blame you. But I don't think you are the kind who gives up so easily."

Guilt pulled up the hairs on the back of her neck as she surveyed the patch of ground beneath her with its dry earth and stones.

"You can speak at ease with me, Gerwalta," Igor continued. "Tell me, what are your thoughts?"

"My thoughts?" She managed her feet, despite the awkward gyrating required by her belly. "I crave raw meat and silver is poison to me. What do you think my thoughts should be?"

"That you don't understand what you are anymore, let alone who."

His accuracy hit her hard, making her blink in surprise.

Igor grinned as he offered her a hand and helped her to navigate her way off the ledge and back into the building. "Don't forget, unlike lupines and wolfsretters, vampires aren't born dark ones; we are dragged into this world by makers, sometimes against our will. The first time I thirsted for a good man's blood, I was just as confused and perplexed as you're likely feeling now."

"And what did you do about it?"

"I found a monk in a dark corner of an abbey and drank my fill."

She didn't know if Igor had meant the statement as a jest, though the light tone suggested it, but she couldn't bring herself to find its humor.

"That is different," Gerwalta persisted. "What you were driven to do was necessary to continue living. But this... I can tolerate and perhaps even understand craving unusual food. When Zelda was expecting the first time, she briefly had a taste for pine sap. But I am a wolfsretter; silver has answered my call since I stepped out of my sacred fire. Now it turns against me, as though I was nothing more than a..."

She cut herself off.

"Nothing more than a werewolf," Igor finished for her. Her guilty eyes confirmed it. "There is no sin in the fear that you'll assume another's weakness. But I'm certain your current condition isn't your condition at all; it's the child's. For the moment, her blood is your blood, thus the inversion."

"But does that mean my child... my child...will be harmed by the very element which gives me strength? How can such a child possibly thrive in our world?"

The vampire shrugged. "Perhaps it cannot."

"Igor!"

"What? I'm not saying the child will die. I am merely saying that, perhaps, the kind of life you'll give your daughter will need to be very different from what you and Andreas envision."

Gerwalta shook her head. "If she is susceptible to silver in utero, there is no way she'll thrive without a pack. Survive, perhaps, but I don't believe it'll be good for her. For the moment, she and Andreas have bonded, saving him from lunacity nonetheless, but if something were to ever happen to him... Wait!"

Gerwalta stopped in her steps and turned to her host. "You said 'daughter' distinctly. Are you... Do you have anyway of..."

"It is my belief that you carry a girl," Igor confirmed. "I suspect Andreas knows as well, but so many men want of men simply because they are men. There is no scent of anything male about you. Except occasionally on your person when you come from your room too hastily."

She fought the blush filling her cheeks.

Igor gently nudged her with his shoulder as they walked. "Stop. There is no shame in partaking of the blessings marriage affords."

"I've no shame. Only..." She exhaled, preparing to unravel the last layer of her unease for the vampire to examine. "Do you know why I rushed from the kitchens just now? Because for the first time, I realize what a selfish thing it was for me to wed Andreas. I don't mean because it took my mother's heir from her or the king from his pack. There will always be another to fill that void. But..." Her hands smoothed down over her child just as the halfling kicked within her. "She will be the one who truly feels the consequences of our apostasy. What right did I have to create such a tempest of an inheritance for so innocent a creature?"

"Frau Baron, vampires are not soothsayers. We cannot see the future, but I cannot believe fate would so haphazardly marry your fortunes only to turn a blind eye to the fruit of your union. Don't think of the legacy you'll leave as a burden. You are two creatures who defied the bigoted traditions of your people to embrace something bigger than rules and races: your love. Would that all children could claim such lofty pedigrees, I feel this world would be a much better place."

At that, the vampire offered his arm. "Now, I've not had much experience with expectant mothers, either as a human or a vampire, but I do recall, one is to indulge their appetites. If your daughter wants fresh meat, let's make sure she gets some before Antoine cuts that ox into something fit for cooking. I'm quite certain we can procure a knife made of lesser metals."

She accepted his arm. "Was Andreas terribly disturbed when I rushed out?"

"Not so much as Antoine."

"But why?"

"Because he was left alone with Andreas."

TWELVE

The messenger clutched the letter in one hand while vaguely holding out another. Inga considered killing him. She'd killed others for less insolent misdeeds than expecting payment. In addition, who asked payment from a nun? True, Inga wasn't a member of the order. She was hiding out here, pretending to make penance as her father demanded, waiting out her sentence until Igor thought she'd suffered enough or until a better opportunity made itself clear.

But must that include payment for services like some common pauper?

At last, she huffed and pulled a gold coin from the small purse tied at her waist, slipping it into the messenger's hand. "Meet me here again before dawn, in case I have to send a reply." Bodies created problems, no matter how much blood you drained from them.

"Of course, Sister, it would be my delight."

With the boldness of a musk ox, the merchant took up the hand Inga used to take the letter and kissed it. Some men enjoyed tempting the sisters. The insolent cur indeed flared temptation within her, but not the sort for which he hoped. She'd let him live tonight, but she might take something more precious than his blood come morning.

The moment she was out of sight of the main hall, Inga broke the seal—the one that had been hers not even a year ago—and unfurled the parchment. The sliver of the moon above provided light, though her sensitive eyes needed even less than that to make out the writing.

I write to acknowledge the receipt of your letter and to tell you for the discussions here at court upon its deliberation. Indeed, you still have friends among the courtesans. Messina di Grecchi in particularly spoke at some length in favor of your petition. However, it is my decision as Doge which I write to share with you.

Your request for a pardon of your crimes against Venice has been denied. This isn't to say that you might not one day find yourself in our illustrious Republic, but at present, the injury caused to influential members of the court at the fangs of your guests, the Ravens, as well as the significant uptick in deaths caused by their ravenous appetites and the subsequent suspicions of the laity of our presence, mean that the wounds are still too fresh to be cut again. In a few decades, I'll reassess if enough time has passed and enough of the hatchet been buried that you may once again—

"Damn you, Massimo!"

Inga threw the paper on the ground and proceeded to stomp it, a flattened effigy of her former lover-turned-usurper. How dare he? How dare he? A curse upon the court of Massimo Brunneli. Didn't he remember that it was she who elevated him to the role of her royal consort? And now, he was offering favors to her even to consider if she may return in a few decades! What was she supposed to do until then, while away her existence in pestilent Navarre?

It wasn't that Basque country was without charm, but it wasn't Venice. It wasn't at the core of everything fashionable, powerful, and delicious.

It wasn't, frankly, good enough for her.

THIRTEEN

Only the cracking of bones and scrapping of plates broke the silence.

Helga wore a mask of indifference, a dam behind which her frustration built. Across the table, Mehmet's face curdled, the black hood pushing bits of boar about his plate before finally dropping his fork and huffing.

"Can you Germans eat nothing but pork?"

No one spoke, for the Matron sat at the end of the table. Instead, they left it to her to dictate a reaction to the ungracious, overstayed guest.

Gunda took time working through a mouthful of meat. "We are hunters, Mehmet, and what this land provides to us in this season is boar. If you don't like it—"

"It is haram," he broke in. "Unclean! The House of Night doesn't partake of pig, for it was commanded—"

"I won't force you to eat our food." Gunda recaptured control of the conversation with brisk tones. "If you are to be one of us, you must partake like one of us. Or are our offerings and hospitality not enough for you?"

His expression flattened as his head dipped into his chest. He could not take another night bound in irons as punishment. He needed to woo Helga behind closed doors to keep her favor and that was not done from the dungeon. "My apologies, Matron, it wasn't my intention to... Forgive me."

An acidic glare stayed fixed on his as Helga leisurely drew a pull of her wine. Wine he would not touch, because it too was forbidden. Finally, the platitudes came. "No insult taken, Herr Siyah." The dripping, fatty meat slid off the fork and into her mouth. "But so as not to further upset you by forcing you to dine with us at this unclean table, you have my permission to leave."

Anger boiled beneath the surface, threatening to break out across his face and his speech. Mehmet clenched his teeth as he pushed out from the table, bowed to the Matron, and gave Helga one last reproachful scowl, as if to say, you see, this is what I was talking about.

His footsteps could not be fast enough. He wanted to hit something, to yell at the top of his lungs and vent his fury. He'd gambled when he'd left for Venice, aiming for a path into the House of Red... an outcast, exiled. He'd never considered that he may lose his bet and end up without a wife, without a clan, and worse, without power.

In short order, Mehmet found himself outside the castle, through the baileys, and out the east gate. He jumped, smacking Andreas Baron's severed hand, hung on the outer wall of the Schloss as a warning to any other wolfsretter-fancying lupines. It swung on an arc behind him as Mehmet threw back his head and bellowed into the night.

"That smug, arrogant, ungracious... bitch!"

Passion trumped wisdom, and the moment the word escaped his lips, Mehmet threw his hands over his mouth. He had to stay focused, stay contained. Helga was his last chance at redemption. By now, his story had filtered out to all the European houses, the betrothed fiancé of the Red Matron's fourth daughter, abandoned at the tent. Even dark ones loved gossip. He was wed, but unwed. Trapped into a marriage that had never been consummated, and thus, in an odd limbo between the two. He couldn't arrange another marriage unless either his fiancé died or the matron of her clan absolved his obligation. Gunda Faust would not allow the latter, and had refused to secure the former, choosing to exile her daughter instead and only slay the wolf with whom she sinned.

Helga must become matron, release him of his obligation to Gerwalta, and accept him into her clan, or the only choice left to him would be heading east into the Caucasus. Or worse still, the New World.

He'd rather die.

But after the bold acts of setting up her husband to be slain, Helga refused to advance on the throne. "I know my mother and the mood of the court," she'd said, "and I will act when I am certain I can do so with my family's support." So again, Mehmet was obliged to wait on the determination of willful women. With a huff, he schooled his features and turned back to the castle. If he hoped to keep that chance alive, he needed to be ready to entertain Helga when she called upon him at dawn. Mehmet took one last look at the swinging hand, offering the slain lupine's hand a silent curse, when he saw that there was no hand.

But there was a paw.

Mehmet blinked. Rubbed his eyes. Looked again. Saw the same.

Impossible. That's all he could think. Impossible. Once a werewolf died, even if it should happen whilst he was in his fur, his body—or any portion thereof—reverted to a laymen's form with the rising of the sun. It did not change postmortem. It could not change.

Unless...

Unless, perhaps, the wolf from whom the paw had come...

...wasn't dead.

Helga waited until the sun peaked over the edge of the horizon and the rest of the household had descended into sleep to sneak into Mehmet's room.

"My love..." He stood to greet her, arms open.

Helga delivered punishment in the form of an open hand across his cheek. "Fool!" she growled as he spun. "She can kill you, you know? My mother will throw away your life as easily as a pebble in her boot. If you die, then everything I've sacrificed for us will have been in vain!"

Clutching the patch of skin which bloomed blue, Mehmet rose to his feet. "What you have sacrificed? You gave up a husband you didn't care for and a sister you detested. I've abandoned my homeland and my chance at marrying an uçan, all to prostrate myself before your beast-loving, lying betrayer of a mother."

"Lying?" The accusation came out of nowhere, a cannonball which hit Helga's walls and left a hole. "What are you talking about?"

Mehmet turned and crossed the room to where a basket lay atop a table. Whatever he drew from it was no bigger than a fist but concealed inside a slip of cloth. He laid the object in her open hand, helping her to pull off the wrapping.

"A paw?" Her face screwed up. "But... the nerves and vessels are dry. This isn't a new injury. Or is it a natural wolf, not a lupine at all?"

"It is werewolf, but as you say, not a new injury."

She turned the ghastly object over in her hand. "A severed limb this old should have reverted to a laymen state by now. How is it still like this?"

"It is not how you should ask," Mehmet said as he took the paw back, wrapping the linen back about it and hiding it away. "Rather, ask me whose paw it is."

All Helga had to offer was a blank stare. "I don't understand."

Mehmet closed in, playing with the buttons of the red hood's tunic. "Do you think your mother's betrayal of her house and clan would put the court on your side?" He lowered his head, pulling kisses up her neck, before pausing and turning his head. "Why is the hand your mother brought as proof of Baron's execution suddenly a paw if its owner is dead?"

Helga tilted her head to the side as Mehmet's hand slipped under her tunic. "That is Barron's hand?"

"His paw, his hand." Mehmet laughed. "Don't you see, Helga? This is it. This is what you needed to finally seize the throne."

But her heart refused to accept it just because it was a

convenient turn of events. She could believe Gerwalta's betrayal; the youngest daughter of the clan had always been the least fervent in her loyalties. But her mother, the matron herself?

Mehmet pressed a hand to her cheek. "Do you not believe me? If you want, we can go now outside the outer walls. You'll see Baron's hand no longer there."

"I believe it is his, but how would we even begin to convince my siblings and my father? My mother will merely say it is not so, and they wouldn't dare to call her liar without better proof than a magically shifting paw. It could be anyone's paw."

Mehmet's eyebrow arched. "What sort of proof?"

Her breath hitched as he picked her up and walked her to the bed, her legs weaving around his waist. "We need him. But my mother wouldn't let any one of us go without cause, and trying to keep such a secret, she will not be eager to give leave."

The wolfsretter of the House of Night was dark in all the beautiful ways his bloodline allowed. Black eyes, tanned skin, curly ebony locks. He looked like the midnight sky made flesh as he hovered over her on the bed. "Matron Faust refuses to release me from my marriage contract with Gerwalta, and in doing so, she's given me all the reason I need to go. I am only attempting to win back my bride."

"But where will you go? You don't even know where to find them."

"Of course, I do. She will have gone to the only place that would put her under the aegis of someone as powerful as your mother. She's gone to Karahan, and Karahan is in Navarre."

She buried a laugh into his neck. "As if you are privy to the movements of so illustrious a vampire."

"I am not, but I did not squander my time in Venice. I have ears in the court. I've been told that the new Doge recently received a message from Karahan's daughter, Inga, from Navarre. He will not be far from her, I can guarantee it. I will go there under the guise of reclaiming Gerwalta, and instead drag back Baron in chains."

Yes, that could work, Helga thought. "Then leave come nightfall.

But for now—" She bucked her hips up, joining them together in their bedroom dance. "—your night belongs to me."

FOURTEEN

Few were the men who could truthfully claim they had surprised a vampire with their approach, fewer still that were left alive to tell the tale.

Mehmet Siyah of the House of Night nodded when their eyes met as though they were old friends. Igor's hands clenched so tightly, he wondered if his fingernails would be bloody should he lift his hand. The petite señorita he'd been charming followed his gaze, in the act of giving Igor an eyeful of that beautiful neck stretched long. His fangs burst forth of their own volition. He'd been foolish to go so long without feeding, but he feared what might happen if he left Andreas and Gerwalta unprotected. So far, he'd succeeded at keeping their presence concealed from other dark ones. If anyone understanding the significance of that child should learn of its imminent birth... He hesitated to think of the devious sort of aged vampire that would like nothing more than to have a youth-bestowing blood creature in his stable.

Igor leaned in and took the peasant girl's hand, raising it to his lips to lay a gentle kiss. He bit back his desires, both for the blood and for her body, and mumbled his apologies. "A moment, dulcinea, but someone needs to see me urgently."

By the time he'd made his way across the partially filled tavern, Mehmet had settled himself at a table, his black cloak pooling around his person.

Igor assumed the seat across from him. "The locals would think you a priest if you had a white collar and any sanctity to speak of."

"Do you say that because I am a Muslim?"

"No, I say that because you are a scoundrel." Igor leaned forward. "It has been two centuries since this land was taken back from the Moors, but be warned, Siyah, some have not let it go. I doubt as though Andreas Baron will take your arrival well, either."

The wolfsretter wove his fingers together as he planted his elbows on the table. "You give away your secrets, Karahan."

"I give away nothing you don't already know," Igor replied. "There would be no reason for you to be here unless you knew."

"I respect that you aren't the type of man who—what is this saying, beats around the bush?" Mehmet lowered his hands and leaned forward. "Are they still in residence?"

"Yes, and if you know anything of my reputation and capabilities, you would do best to take that answer with you to Constantinople. You tried playing the situation with the Ravens to your advantage and failed. Take what remains of your pride and crawl back in search of your imaginary lost pack of the Golden Horn."

The smirk across the other man's face flattened. "They are real, and someday they'll slip up and trust in someone or something they shouldn't. And when they do, the House of Night will be there to smite them and their anathema queen."

Igor rolled his eyes. He'd never understand the rigidity that lupines and wolfsretters alike had about the agency of the two sexes.

"Nevertheless, I've abandoned that quest, and sought more… fruitful opportunities."

Mehmet moved with a speed the quickest vampire would appreciate. One moment he sat, relaxed and nonchalant. The next, he'd drawn—or given the talents of his kind, perhaps, created—a silver blade out of thin air. The dagger plunged into Igor's left hand, severing flesh and bone.

The laity about them revealed themselves for the cattle they were. The herd was spooked, and spooked herds ran. Within moments they were alone.

Good, fewer witnesses that way. Perhaps that had been the hood's intention. Igor had underestimated Mehmet's schemes once; he was not eager to do it again.

Igor looked up to Mehmet who, a credit to him, wore smugness instead of surprise. No doubt the wolfsretter thought such an act would have more of an effect, or he'd not have undertaken it. "What is it you're after now?"

"The wolf. You'll deliver him to me tonight or the next cut will be to your spine."

Straight-faced, Igor examined the inflicted hand. The pain was minimal. The blood loss, insignificant. "What claim is it you believe you have to him?"

"Gerwalta is my wife by contract if not yet consummated in flesh, and that wolf practically stole her from our marital bed. Don't pretend you're unaware that by our laws that is a capital offense."

What an annoying little pissant. No wonder his own clan had sent him packing.

"I know what your laws state, but they came to me seeking sanctuary. Why would I betray them like that?"

Mehmet folded his arms across his chest and sat back in his chair. "Remind me what it was that you originally went to Triberg to inquire about? Some sort of safekeeping of your shame?"

Every nerve in the vampire's body pulsed. "You wouldn't."

Mehmet rubbed his chin. "Tell me, Karahan, why should the wolfsretter be the guardians of the vampires' refuse? What offense did the Ravens ever commit against us?"

"Even you couldn't be that foolish. If the Ravens go free, the first person on their kill list will be the wife you claim you want to rescue."

Mehmet's eyes went wide. "Did I say anything to imply I cared what becomes of Gerwalta after my use of her passes?"

Igor swallowed down his hate. Rage would not serve him now. "If the Ravens are released back into the world, it won't only cost the dark ones dearly. They'll mobilize their alliances in the east and attempt to overthrow the laity courts, just as they had been working towards before. Thousands, perhaps millions will die." Keeping his anger from boiling over grew more difficult with each word. Clutching the edge of the table, Igor's fingernails splintered wood. "Are you so blinded by your own ambitions that you'd release death upon humanity? The Matron looked the other way and let Barron go, why can't you?"

"It is you, not I, who will determine if that comes to pass."

Igor shook his head. "I won't give up Gerwalta."

"But the wolf? Come now, what would she need him for? I imagine by now, she's taken his seed." Mehmet drew a lazy pattern over the table, even as Igor's jaw dropped. "Let's not pretend that she's a shy and reserved woman. I had anticipated that my wife, properly wooed, would be overtly encouraging of bed sport and wolfsretters are known for their bountiful fertility."

As though lightning had struck Igor's body, his spine went rigid. "Have rumors spread?"

"Rumors would suggest something happened to know about. You've been playing the long game on this one. I know why you conceal her, and I know why you risked all to extract the two of them from their clan and pack and why now you've brought them here to guard. That baby's blood... It would be quite valuable to the right vampire, wouldn't it?"

Curse the eastern hoods and their access to ancient knowledge. "A single drop more precious than that of ten laymen."

Mehmet stood. "I'll be in the vicinity of this tavern tomorrow at this time. Produce the wolf and I'll let you keep Gerwalta."

"And the babe?"

Mehmet swished his hand through the air dismissively. "It has no place in our world but the grave. Do with it what you like." The wolfsretter turned to go. "I make for Triberg tomorrow, and it will either be with the wolf, or with word to the Matron that your contract to house the Ravens is void. The choice is yours."

When Inga's father arrived just as the sun crested the sky and the chants of morning prayer had echoed away, she knew there was something wrong.

The vampire leapt to her feet when he burst into her chamber, having just laid off her habit for the day. "What has happened?"

The words never came. Igor crossed the chamber, pulling her into his arms, her cheek pressed to his chest.

"Father, you are worrying me," she muttered. "It is already dawn. I was about to smoke into the catacombs for the day. Come with me, or hurry home before it is too late."

"It may be too late already. What he says and what he intends to do may be two very different things."

"What who will do?" The words made little sense. "If someone is threatening you, let me leave this place to stand at your side."

Igor's eyes went wide as he pulled back, staring at her like she'd just said the most ridiculous thing imaginable. "No. Stay here. Don't leave the monastery except to go to day rest until my return. Drink from the sisters if you must, but don't leave. I'll be gone no more than a fortnight. I should be able to do it in that time."

"Do what? Father, what is going on?"

"The less I tell you, the safer you are. I just... I feared how much he knew, for he shouldn't have known of any of it, but he somehow did."

"You're not making any sense."

Igor kissed her forehead. "I know, love, I know. I promise, one day I'll tell you. For now, stay and pray. Pray especially for me, that I can save us all from the mess I've made of things. Just know that I have solutions in the works, a way to assure that we'll endure and that you and I both will still be alive to see the end of this. I promise, Inga, all will be well. Just trust me."

"Of course, I do, but I still have no idea what you're talking about."

He squeezed her shoulder. "To your rest, and I to my labor. I love you, and I'll count the moments until my return and our reunion."

And with that, her father smoked out of sight.

FIFTEEN

Why were wolfsretters not partakers of grand literature?

It wasn't that they were an illiterate culture by any means. Gerwalta, like her siblings before her, had been made to learn letters and numbers, as well as French, Latin, and Greek. While the shapes of the Roman tongue had always escaped her mastery, she had read books, but never without intent. All the Faust children studied Machiavelli (in French, as it were) in some depth. But never had Gerwalta had the opportunity to read something merely for pleasure.

At least if their departure for England had been delayed until after the baby was born, Andreas spooked by her fainting spell, she could fill the time with so, so many books.

She lowered the copy of the German translation of Don Quixote Igor had gifted her and sighed as the swell of her belly began to dance. A hand placed against it landed just in time to receive a swift kick.

"Definitely a girl," she said to herself. "And definitely eager not to be in there anymore." She observed the room around her at large, trying to recall the last time she'd felt at ease anywhere else but here. "I can sympathize, little bug."

Thoughts of her child and her longings for the forest flitted away as Andreas swept into the room, a mask of apprehension on his face. She tried to shoot to her feet, but what ensued instead was a comical balancing act between the realm of the possible and practical. She finally achieved a standing position after several modifications to both style and form.

"Is something the matter, love?"

Bless her mate, he didn't say a thing about her awkward composure. "Igor has left."

"Left? To go where?"

"He wouldn't say." Andreas turned to peek back into the hall before closing their door. "He said he would return within a fortnight, and that we were to remain here and to be certain that we didn't venture outside the castle, not even at night and not even on its own grounds. The laity staff remain to serve us, but the castle has no lord."

The great dragon whose presence warded off any interloper had flown. But while that seemed at face value to open them to danger, Gerwalta had to remind her spouse of the obvious. "We've been here for months without the least sign of danger. No one knows of us. Well, except for the laymen in Igor's employ, but surely you don't fear their disloyalty. It would cost them their own livelihoods, not to mention in all likelihood, their lives."

"I don't fear the servants; I question the intentions of the master."

An odd pang tightened in her abdomen, making Gerwalta bend slightly. "Igor? But he's been nothing but hospitable and welcoming since the moment we arrived."

"True, but have you noticed how concerned he is that we'll be seen, or how he never asked about our decision to leave and why we never acted on it after your silver sickness?"

"I presume he wishes us to stay to provide distraction. Have you noticed how isolated he is? Vampires favor grand cosmopolitan cities because of the excitement and activity. The village barely tops Triberg in those ways. I suspect he's here until the consequences of Venice shake out, and he's starved of entertainment. Even if his reasons are selfish in that way, Andreas, there is no crime in enjoying the company of guests. Surely, you're not saying that Igor is plotting in the shadows against us? To what end? We can offer him nothing."

Andreas's eyes cast down Gerwalta's frame. "He has made himself overly interested in your comfort and the baby's wellbeing. He has never treated me poorly, but he often only addresses me as an afterthought. I have to wonder if..."

"You suppose he has some cruel intention for our child." Gerwalta cut him.

"I don't know that it is cruel, but I don't know that it necessarily involves us," he said. "Gerwalta, have you ever asked yourself why the asenaic and his mate we met in Venice never arrived in Triberg?"

"We don't know that they didn't," she countered. "Mehmet said that they were on their way, that they were awaiting my wedding festivities to slip into the packlands without the Matron's notice whilst all in the schloss were distracted. And then you and I... well, mated and fled right after that."

Andreas shook his head. "I cannot be without my doubts. We do know that it was Igor who helped them flee Constantinople. We've only Mehmet's claims of that. It's made me wonder why a vampire would care what happened to an asenaic?"

Doubt furrowed her brow. "You're attempting to build castles out of field stones."

"And what of the Doge?" Andreas continued, undeterred. "Bianca? Inga? She went by both names, depending on who was concerned, as I recall. She is here in Navarre somewhere; I've overheard the servants mention her, but Igor never has. Don't you find that bizarre?"

What she found was this sudden suggestion of conspiracy inconvenient. Why must wolves always circle prey? Why could they not just attack head-on? "Perhaps vampires just keep their own counsel."

Andreas shook his head. "Something isn't adding up. Gerwalta, my duty as your mate is to protect you and our baby at all costs, and I'm no longer certain this is still the best place to do that."

In an instant, Gerwalta cupped her hands over his sole remaining one. "Then we go."

"Just like that? I say I've a suspicion and you resolve to let go your own?"

"It is the most efficient way to address your concerns. Besides," she said, "even if I don't share them, I trust your insight. You were a king. Perhaps only of a small pack in the Schwarzwald, but that made you privy to seeing things others wished you not to. If your instincts tell you something is afoot, then it may be."

"Then we go tomorrow at dawn," he said, pushing a kiss unto

her cheek. "I'll see what provisions I can scrounge up; you do the same. We must travel light and with the sun, so that if Igor is indeed planning something, he'll be powerless to pursue us."

That part, however, seemed wrong to her. "As impacted as we will be by my condition, isn't it best we travel at night, when we are stronger?"

Andreas lifted his missing appendage, gesturing as though his left hand was still present. "I am a wolf without a paw and you are a wolfsretter who cannot control silver. Outside of our ability to scent and see better than the laity, night gives us little advantage now. Besides, in the day we'll have an easier time blending in among other travelers."

"And our destination? Does it remain unchanged?"

Andreas nodded. "Yes, we need to make England, and soon. Our child will come with the next full moon."

SIXTEEN

The vampire was so predictable. Or better yet, he was so manipulatable.

Mehmet knew the moment he suggested the Raven's jars could be expelled from the custodianship of the House of Red that the thought would fester in Karahan's head. What a shame that vampires couldn't simply kill off their misguided progeny. Not only did it esure their mistakes would come back to haunt them, it also gave others a weakness to exploit. Mehmet found a gathering of large boulders not far from the entry to Karahan's property, a place where shadow gave him cover, and waited.

Night passed, and the black hood had begun to think he'd miscalculated. He was about to bed down for the day when he heard it: his betrothed's voice approaching.

Wonderful, he thought. Late, but still as predicted. Now that the cat had run, all Mehmet need do was wait to see the mice scurry.

And that was the thing about mice. They always scurried.

"Andreas!"

He jolted awake at the sound of his name. "What? What is it? I'm awake. I'm awake."

Gerwalta, through some laborious twisting, maneuvered herself on to the bench beside him. The hay cart wasn't the finery his mate deserved, but in pressed moments and with no other options, it was the one Andreas could offer.

"You're sleep deprived and overly taxed from doing too much

72

with too little time." She took the leather straps from his hand. "Go, rest. I'll drive some distance."

Though he surrendered the horses to her, his mind still rebelled. "I'll lay down, but I'll stay awake."

"How do you propose to do that? You can't even stay awake sitting up." She jerked her head to the bed of grass behind them. "I'll rouse you when I stop midday to water the horses."

"And if there is any danger..." His voice trailed off, even as he crawled over the wall of the hay bin and began to pull and push the dry grass to suit his comfort.

"What danger could there be? Even a highwayman wouldn't be so cruel as to attack a woman in my condition."

The cart emerged from a patch of low-rise forest. Mehmet pulled his silver from concealment beneath his cloak, used it to tip the arrow shaft, and nocked it onto the string of his bow.

Pull, aim, release.

Direct hit.

His feet flew, eating up the ground. Blood scented the air. Lupine blood. The arrow vibrated with each flail Baron made, its head buried deep in his left thigh. The wolf wailed, screamed, bellowed... all driving the horses to distraction. The two meager beasts bucked, throwing the frame of the cart onto which they were attached flying.

Gerwalta grabbed a sword from the hay and swung out before her, unleashing the shocked creatures who wasted no time in running off. As his betrothed turned to aid the wolf, Mehmet saw it... the evidence of her advanced condition. Until that moment, he thought he didn't care what happened to her, nor did he take any offense for her infidelity. But seeing the proof made plain, anger flared within. Mehmet detested her not because she had betrayed him, but because she had betrayed her own kind.

"Traitor!" He pressed on with lopped steps as the balance of his silver formed the scimitar in his hands. "Befouled and wretched creature!"

Gerwalta spun, all the color from her puffy face fading at the sight of him. "You!"

She left her mate to bleed, knowing the shot that had landed must be painful, but not deadly. That didn't mean that Mehmet had missed his target. With silver embedded beneath the lupine's skin, Andreas Baron would find taking his fur impossible. The wound was calculated only to keep him human.

"How dare you!" Gerwalta shouted.

"How dare I?" Mehmet returned, raising the sword. "How dare you? You leave me at our wedding fire to open your legs to this putrid creature? You killed one of your own clan to protect his dirty pack? You Jezebel. I should slay you both for this treachery."

The lupine struggled to turn over, anchoring himself on all fours, looking for a moment very much like a layman imitating the wolf he could become. And then Mehmet saw it: the reason he struggled to find balance.

In addition to the arrow wound, of course.

"Missing a paw, Andreas?" Mehmet mocked. "Don't fret. We have it waiting for you back in Triberg."

Gerwalta stopped dead where she stood. "Andreas, run!" The red hood raised her sword, ready to strike if Mehmet came closer. "Stand down. I will kill him before I let you drag him back in chains. That is your plan, isn't it? Use him to implicate my mother, give Helga all the evidence she needs to kill two birds with one stone."

"You're as wise as you are depraved." Mehmet lifted his silver. "You could have been an empress among my people and yours, and you gave it all away to become this cur's bitch. You don't deserve a reprieve, Gerwalta. You die now."

The wolf called out as Mehmet swung and his love fell to the ground. Moments later, the black wolfsretter turned his attention back.

It took only one hard knock upon the head to render him

unconscious. His massive body would take hours to drag back to town.

Luckily, somewhere near, there was a cart with two horses ready to go.

SEVENTEEN

Hunger sparked by the delicious scent took Inga's body hostage.

Blood had been spilt. Fresh, warm, oozing blood. Blood that would slake her thirst and fuel her powers and drive her to the edges of carnal satisfaction.

Blood, blood, blood...

Her fangs dropped into place of their own volition even as she steadied herself against a wall. A hand shot up to hide the evidence of her condition, even as one of the sisters rushed past her.

"Sister Maria Dominga?" Inga forced her teeth to retract just as the small, young nun came to a stop and turned. "What has happened? Is it one of the sisters? Someone is injured badly."

Maria Dominga grinned. "You truly are blessed by the Creator. His gifts are strong in your veins."

Not as strong as they would be if I drank you dry.

No, penance. You are here to do penance. Venice has rejected you, you have nowhere else to go. Father will find out if you kill anyone, then you'll end up just like the Ravens, sealed in silver until the end of time.

Igor was fair, but once one of his children crossed a line, he was also cruel. The paterfamilias of the Dracule bloodline could have easily exchanged favors with that of another and had Vlad and his sycophants killed. Instead, he'd forced them to endure, deprived, powerless, alone to contemplate their misdeeds until at last, they surrendered to the sun or just faded away encased in silver.

"A traveler found a woman on the side of the road," Maria Dominga continued, bringing Inga back to the moment. "Poor thing is beaten something dreadful, stabbed and left for dead. It is only by some miracle she survived. Mother Superior and Sister Maria Inez are doing what they can, but the injuries are quite..."

Inga's thoughts turned to the benefits of magnanimity, of how proud her father would be if she could offer aid in the face of utter temptation. Perhaps even proud enough that he'd think her debt to the laity balanced and allow her to leave the convent.

"I'll help." She drove forward, past the nascent nun. There was no need to inquire where the beaten woman was; a vampire's thirst drew her to wherever that glorious liquid pooled over fresh wounds.

Maria Dominga scurried after her. "Yes, perhaps our Lord will continue to work miracles through you. Perhaps you can help save her."

The moment Inga saw the bruised and bloodied creature, however, she knew that even God would be challenged. The sisters had stripped the woman of her clothing, allowing access to wounds that started at the top of her head and continued down to her ankles. Patches of red and blue bloomed across her arms, her legs, her back. Red hair, matted with dried blood and dirt, hung in clumps. Black eyes floated in a swollen mask of pain above a busted lip and bloody nose. Just beneath one breast, Inga saw where a section of skin was missing. Stabbed wasn't quite the right word, for that would imply a blade had entered her person. Whomever had tried for that had missed, cutting down the poor creature's side but not entering the body cavity.

And how she bled...

In the oddest of all circumstances, that wound, unlike the others around it, looked singed. Had whatever rapscallion that attacked her burned her as well? A pregnant woman? If Inga knew the bastard's identity, she'd personally rip off his arms and filet his gullet.

"Rosaria!"

The vampire snapped to attention at the utterance of her alias. "Yes, Mother Superior?"

"Clean cloths." The elderly nun's eyes and attention had already turned back to the victim who, Inga would credit, was doing her best to breathe through the pain. "Whatever happened, it has the baby thinking it might be time to exit. Inez, ask the other sisters to pray. After we dress the wounds, her fate will be in bigger hands than ours."

The battered creature on the table muttered something, but the language was neither Basque nor Spanish. Mother Superior, who only could hold a passable conversation in the former, leaned in. "What dear?"

"She's speaking French," Inga informed while translating. "She's asking if anyone has found her husband."

"I see." Mother Superior paused from cleaning the side wound to push the woman's hair off her face. "Tell her, Rosaria, that we didn't know to look but we'll send word to the village near where she was found to inquire. Tell her to give us a name and a description of him."

Delirium transformed the woman's words into something not entirely intelligible. Inga translated what she could. "His name is... Wolfson? He's missing a..." Inga paused to ask if she had properly understood, then continued when the woman managed a nod. "He only has one hand. The right one."

Mother Superior grimaced. "Was that before or after they were attacked?"

But the answer would have to wait. With a groan, the woman sighed and slipped into unconsciousness.

"Just as well." Mother Superior rose to her feet, gathering up a handful of saturated rags before dropping them into a dish of crimson-stained water which she shoved into Inga's chest. "She won't need any translating while she's out. Get fresh cloths and hot water and hurry."

Inga stood transfixed. The blood... it was just there, in her hands. Diluted in water, perhaps, but still fresh, still warm even. Her father hadn't given her leave to drink from the nuns, but was someone under their care that different? All she had to do was...

"Rosaria!"

"Yes, at once." Inga turned and ran as quickly as she could without spilling the bowl's contents, and without attracting attention. When she found herself outside, the light of a half-moon beaming down, she couldn't quite remember how she'd gotten there.

The stars danced, reflecting against the blood-laced water. Tears formed in the corner of her eyes. It was barbaric, beneath her, but how long had it been? Her father fed her his own blood on his visits. It kept her alive, the secondhand life in his veins stolen from others infusing her body with just enough strength to endure, but she'd been starving for months. Igor split hairs; the victim being treated inside wasn't of the monastery. If she drank, Igor would consider that a violation of his trust. But how could he learn of this? What evidence would there be if she partook of this fortuitous offering?

Inga squeezed out the rags, thickening the brew, before tossing them aside. The sweet and savory scent pulled at her senses as she lifted the bowl, bringing it to the rim of her bottom lip. The bouquet... It was different somehow, more tart. But blood was blood was blood, and she hadn't had nearly enough of it in so very long. She tipped up the bowl and...

"No!"

An arc of red shone for a flicker of a moment, catching the rays of the moon above. Inga fell to her knees, pressing the grounded liquid into the dirt, willing it to soak into the soil more quickly. She wouldn't betray her father. She wouldn't quench her thirst with the spilt blood of an innocent mother-to-be. She wouldn't become the monster they all had said she was.

Determination stiffened her steps and quickened her pace as she resumed a place at Mother Superior's side, a pile of clothing in her hands. The beaten woman had come to—conscious but trancelike. She'd either been trained to hide injury or had been injured enough in her lifetime to know how to masque pain. It was a warrior's tactic, but what kind of woman would receive such an education? The laity did not send their women to battle.

It was then that the terrible thought entered Inga's head. Had the woman said her husband was named Wolfson, or that he was a wolf's son?

All the color drained from Inga's face as she leaned in to whisper into the woman's ear. "Are you of the dark, child?"

Mother Superior raised an eyebrow. "What are you saying, Rosaria?"

"I am asking if she was attacked after dark," Inga lied. French wasn't Basque, nor was it Spanish, but the tongues twisted together and the best way to conceal the truth was to be in the proximity of it. "If it was day, she might have seen who did it."

Even through busted lips and looking out of bloody, swollen eyes, Inga heard the condemning admission. "Oui, je suis de la nuit."

Inga rose, knowing what she must do, but hating all the same that it must be done. Her father had forbidden her to seek any dark one. Not only vampires, but wolves and wolfsretter alike. Igor's faith in her was so shaken, Inga wasn't sure if he'd believe that a wolfsretter had by chance been brought to her convent. Perhaps he himself had even arranged it, the whole story of his needing to journey suddenly a prologue to a test, a way to see if Inga could be trusted to follow his edicts while he was afar.

She wouldn't fail so easy a test.

When Mother Superior finally deigned to raise her eyes, Inga took the woman under her influence, pushing away her own thoughts. "In the morning, you'll send this woman away from here."

Mother Superior nodded. "Yes, that would be best."

"We'll do what we can to assist her, but she'll be made to leave as soon as she can walk."

The nun's faith was strong, but her mind was weak and easily reshaped. "She is recovering with remarkable speed. A merchant caravan is leaving north tomorrow. We can ask that she be given a place amongst them."

Inga hated herself, now more than ever. "And if anyone is to ask after an injured woman brought here, we'll say she passed away. You'll instruct all the sisters that this is what we'll say."

"We shall say we buried her in the graveyard."

Yes, that would do nicely. "You'll have to be certain the groundman digs a grave then. Her battered clothing should be buried there, and any silver she was carrying."

Little lines formed on Mother Superior's brow. "There was no silver."

What kind of wolfsretter went about without silver, especially while expecting? No wonder she had been bested. In her condition and without any weapons, she would have been an easy kill.

Inga gave one last resolute nod. "And my father will never know I was in the same room with her, nor that I even knew of her presence."

The nun nodded. "As if you were never here."

EIGHTEEN

The castellan came at dawn, just as Gunda had taken off her silver and readied herself for bed. "Can it not wait?"

Therese hesitated before saying in the smallest voice she'd ever used, "I don't think so, your grace."

As the Matron entered the throne room, a slurry of scents washed over her. Blood, sweat, silver, and agony combined to tell a story of suffering. The stench of spoiled meat suggested a wound from a beating that had either been allowed to fester, or freshly opened before it could properly heal. Soon, the source of the stink became apparent. The hobbled lupine wore shredded rags and his own filth for clothing. What concerned Gunda wasn't the fact that a werewolf had been dragged into her presence as a prisoner when she had given no orders for one to be taken. Rather, it was the fact that every member of her clan was present. Both her daughters who remained in Triberg, her son and his wife, the one son-in-law left alive, her husband... And in the midst of them all, holding the silver chain which bound the wolf, the horrible snake who'd slithered his way into her court, the wolfsretter from the House of Night.

Her heart seized. Had he succeeded in tracking down Gerwalta?

Gunda drew to a stop as she focused in on Helga and Zelda standing on the dais, her eyes narrowing. "Who dared to call for a clan gathering in my stead? And why is this one—" She slung a hand in Mehmet's direction. "—returned without Gerwalta? Is that not why he left, to find her?"

"Indeed it is," Mehmet said, turning slowly, "but as it turns out, I found something of greater value than a betraying bride. Would you like to see, Gunda?"

She stomped forward, prepared to give the insolent interloper a lesson with the back of her hand for referring to her in so informal a fashion, when he tugged on the chain and spun the wolf around.

She was ruined.

His eyes were swollen. Deep cuts around his face and neck still glistened with fresh blood. He'd been beaten so closely within an inch of his life, not even his own mother would know the sight of him. But Gunda did.

It was the missing hand that gave it away.

As all the color drained from Gunda's face, Helga stepped to the front of the dais. "Correct me if I'm wrong, Mother, but this is Andreas Baron, is it not? The same Andreas Baron who you said you tracked down and killed? Whose hand you brought back as a trophy? He does appear to be very much alive."

Gunda took one piteous look at the wolf before stumbling toward her eldest. "Helga, please, you—"

No sooner had she gotten the words out than the two male members of her bloodline closed in, taking her by the arms.

"Gunda Faust, I find you guilty," Helga said, passing judgement. "Not only did you lie to us, but you aided and abetted a criminal lupine to escape justice. In doing so, you have become a betrayer. The sentence for such betrayal is death."

Gunda drew in a deep breath, the initial shock turning over into anger. "How dare you! I am the Matron of this house, and it is at my discretion who is punished and for what."

"Your discretion put you in league with our enemies." Her husband's face... Heartbroken. Injured. Forlorn. "Why, my Gundy? Why did you do this to us?"

"I did nothing to you. To any of you." Gunda's head lashed to the right. "Can you not smell the conspiracy cooked up by this usurper? Or did any of you, as did I, write to inquire of the Matron of the House of Night as to why he was purged? Insubordination and insurrection, that's why. Disobeying orders and trying to seek out a pack everyone knows was killed off a century ago!"

Helga bellowed. "A convenient lie and at a desperate moment.

We can believe nothing that comes from your lips. You will wear your scarlet v in blood, and you will bear it with shame, Betrayer."

"I'm not the only one who has betrayed this bloodline." Gunda turned to her power-hungry daughter. "But I am the only one who did it for the right reasons."

Helga's face curled into a smile. "Sealed by her own admission."

"As someday, you shall be sealed by yours," Gunda said. "My crime is that I discovered I loved my children more than I loved power. I only wish I could say the same of them."

Perhaps due to the indirect derision, Maximillian's grip tightened on her arm. "Who'd have thought, my own mother a betrayer? Why? Gerwalta chose her fate willingly, knowing the consequences."

"Perhaps she did," Gunda said. "But her child did not."

The others' eyes widened just as a ripple of understanding went through the room.

"The child will never come to be," Mehmet proclaimed, and she watched with disappointment as the others expressed their relief. "I stabbed it in its mother's womb with silver. The child has been slain."

Gunda buried her head into her chest, trying to hide the tears, even as she shook with silent sobs.

Helga clicked her tongue in disgust. "To the dungeons with her," she said. "To the dungeons with them both."

Moist earth, fungus, the filth of dying creatures...

Moonlight pulled open Gunda's eyes, but it was the scent in the air that stained her dreams with blood. She sat up without urgency. What good would it do to hurry? She was trapped in this tomb of a dungeon. An ability to fly did one little good when imprisoned underground.

Nothing to do but sit, wait, and imagine her impending death.

Then came the sound of metal clinking in the darkness, pulling her gaze into the shadows.

"They've chained you."

"Not in silver," Andreas Baron muttered through swollen lips. "They were wiser than that."

"Of course, they were. I am a Matron. Even if I couldn't touch the silver, if I could see it, I'd control it." She crossed her legs to gather what comfort she could. "They must have been frustrated when you threw yourself over me and took the beating meant for me."

"I owed you my life, what else would I do?"

"Let me die," she said shortly, matter-of-factly. "Let me receive the just punishment for the crimes I myself have committed."

His eyes went to the floor. "Are you angry that I intervened?"

Gunda couldn't help but laugh. "As if that matters now." When she grew somber again, she asked it... the very question of which the answer would legitimize her suffering. "Gerwalta?"

Andreas's eyes lifted. "You heard what Mehmet said."

"And I know you're a mated wolf and would have no reason to live if your mate and your baby were dead," she said. "You weren't my first königswolf, Andreas Baron, even if you were my last."

"Be that as it may, Gerwalta is not a wolf. The bond I have with her... I don't think it works that way."

The Matron said nothing, but she did raise an eyebrow in suspicion.

Andreas's face bunched up, as though he were frustrated to have his secrets revealed. After a moment, he heaved a heavy sigh. "I cannot sense her wellbeing. I wouldn't even know that she still lives, except I know that our child endures. A wolf can sense these things, sense when a close member of his blooded kin passes from this world, no matter the distance."

A queer sense of relief flooded her. It hadn't been until that moment that Gunda Faust herself understood the depth of her concern. "And your brother? Is he still alive?"

Andreas ignored her question, asking instead, "Why aren't they just killing me? I've openly committed the greatest crime your kind prescribes for mine. Even Gerwalta tried to warn me the fate in store if I committed myself to wooing her. Now it is come, why am I unpunished?"

Gunda's strategic mind drew up the likely reason without much work. "Because, Herr Baron, you did not commit the greatest crime, I did. A wolfsretter who loves a wolf... Well, it's an embarrassment, yes, but at the end of the day, her injuries are only to herself and her reputation. But a matron who helps a wolf flee justice? That is why you are still alive. Or should I say... for now."

The lupine shook his head. "I don't understand."

"I am to be executed," Gunda continued. "They await the full moon, when your nature will force you to fur and fury. And then they'll let you lose on me. You see, Andreas, you are the way I die."

She said all this with amusement, and perhaps that's what it was now, amusing. The one thing Gunda knew it wasn't, was avoidable.

"I won't," the wolf suddenly declared. "You saved Gerwalta and me both. As much as I detest you for all the slights you've committed against my people, I refuse to be the cause of your undoing."

Gunda laughed. "Herr Baron, if there is mercy in your soul, I pray that you will be the very thing which ends me. The alternatives will not show me your compassion."

NINETEEN

The last time he'd been at Schloss Wolfsretter, Igor had observed every form of decorum. He sent ahead a messenger to ask formal permission to call. A gift befitting the head of a prominent clan was secured from Munich and presented upon arrival. He'd dressed in his eastern finest so as not to offend the Matron's sensibilities and deferred to her preference in every matter.

Today, Igor observed nothing. He didn't even wait for the gate to be lifted. The vampire became smoke, winding his way around tree and rock, up the mountain from the village through the mist, straight into the heart of the Faust court. He lingered in the shadows until the throne held an occupant, before materializing, fangs bared. "You aren't Matron."

On the throne, the figure wrapped in the traditional red cloak and holding a silver staff glared down at him. "Who are you to say who I am in my own court?"

It took only the space of these words for others in the chamber to rally. He was surrounded, axes and swords and staffs all made of or topped in silver hovered a hair's breadth from his person. The blond woman on the dais, however, took a great amount of leisure in rising to her feet.

"Oh, I know who you are by name," she said. "Goran Karahan, Lord of the Dracule. But what place you think you have in supposing you've any power in this court is presumptive. I am Helga Faust, thirteenth matron of the House of Red. Now, state your business or I'll order your head from your body."

"Try, and I'll delight in personally removing the skin from your exsanguinated corpse."

The red hood bristled. "You have some nerve, Lord Dracule, threatening me in my own court."

"And you've some nerve claiming it as yours," Igor snapped back. He had no time for insolent children. "I come to reaffirm the terms of the contract I made with Gunda Faust last winter."

Helga's eyes rolled to the side, as though looking in the air for answers. "I know of no such agreement."

"Your mother did. She—"

His words cut off as two of the males of the court, one the elder version of the other, raised their silver blades to his throat.

"My mother," Helga said, spitting out the word like a curse, "no longer rules this clan. She lost her position through betrayal, and as such, all contracts she made on behalf of the House of Red are now defunct."

Igor bristled. "Is that the way of it then?"

The wolfsretter nodded. "It is."

"Then bring me the six silver jars. They are my property."

"I'm sorry, but I cannot do that."

"Cannot or will not?" The vampire raised an eyebrow. "Watch yourself on this, Frau Matron. I am attempting patience, but I've never been renown for it."

In a single, swift motion, the wolfsretter leapt from the dais, landing a sword's length from Igor as documented by her suddenly-wrought blade. "This court is aware of the role you played in harboring criminals whose life and fate were forfeit by the weight of their crimes. As such, we could demand restitution, even vengeance. But we did not. We decided to bury your sins with my mother's tenancy and move on. Don't tempt me to reconsider."

If they thought swords would dissuade him from his errand, they were sorely mistaken. Igor glared as he reached out and curled his fingers around the end of Helga's blade. With two steps, he guided it through his ribs, passing just under his heart, all while not flinching a muscle in pain.

Though his blood trickled down over the silver, his countenance remained unwavering. "This is all the effect your weapons have on me." He opened his mouth just as four gleaming fangs sprouted from his gums. "Would you like to see how mine treat you?"

For a spell, Helga stared at the dripping wound on his stomach before pulling back her sword in one rapid pull. The silver flooded its form, melting back into a staff.

"Fine, then," she huffed. "Have it your way."

Igor snapped his fangs back from view. "My property?"

"Maximillian will retrieve the jars." With two snaps, both the men at Igor's sides dropped their weapons, the younger of the two skittering off. "Tell me, Lord Dracule, can I have your word that, without business between us, you'll leave this place and never return?"

"Do I have your word that your clan in turn will not seek me out?" His eyes drifted to the Turk standing at the edge of the room.

Helga flashed an acidic glare at Mehmet before spinning back. "None under my command shall approach you again. If ever the House of Red and the Dracule Bloodline meet, it will be a dark day for us both."

A few minutes later, with the six jars pushed into a large sack and slung over his shoulder, Igor traveled a more conventional route: he walked out the east gate. It was then, on the edge of the bridge that carried one from the keep to the inner bailey, that Igor heard a whimper. With a shift of the wind and a scent upon the air, his senses confirmed it: Andreas Baron was here, and by the sound of it, suffering.

The vampire had given his word, and while the wolfsretters threw such things away at their convenience, a Dracule did not. There had been no fresh scent in the throne room of Gerwalta. In fact, there had been no scent of her anywhere near Triberg. But where would she be if not here?

His feet and heart rebelled. He thought of the baby Gerwalta carried, of the promise of its blood, of the possibilities it held for him and Inga both. An asenaic's blood could sustain a vampire beyond his allotted five hundred years. Igor could still be in the world to assure his demon progeny passed from it, and Inga could be his companion.

But it was more than that selfish care that kept him. Igor

tolerated Andreas, but he liked Gerwalta. More than wish her no harm, he felt an urge to protect her. Perhaps because that had always been his lot: to foster young women exploited by families who didn't value them. He thought of Inga, of how he'd taken her into his clutch and under his protection after Vlad had discarded her. Each time Vlad discarded her. Gerwalta was no less deserving of compassion.

If he dropped the six silver jars, turned, and fought his way into the dungeons, he knew he could defeat any defense the House of Red mounted. But at what cost? Any one of them could melt the jars weighing down his sack and release evil back into the world. How many other lives would his malevolent sons take, just so he could save one wolfsretter?

Igor closed his eyes and whispered a prayer that Andreas's suffering may not be too great. And with that, he left all thoughts of the Barons behind.

TWENTY

Wilhelm knew something was unusual when Herr Minster's cart was heard winding the way up from the village into the packlands, Lisi's form visible even from afar on the bench beside him.

The second-in-command of the Triberg pack had to bite his own tongue to keep his mind focused. His nature called on him to take his fur; four legs would move faster than two along the road. But what would the laymen think of that, seeing an oversized wolf closing in only to shift back to a mortal form to converse politely. And, oh, also the man he would become wouldn't have a stich of clothing on.

Lisi had left for the village at dawn, taking their daughter Jelena; a supply of linen was said to be coming into the market that morning. Little wolves grew fast and sometimes it seemed that Lisi made new unmentionables nonstop. That, or repairing ones their son had torn in his excitement over being old enough to shift. (Lisi made the stiches looser in his things to allow a cleaner, more repairable break.)

Upon approach, his wife's face spoke of nothing but frustration. It was then that Wilhelm felt his heart race a second time. Where was Jelena? Oh, no, what had happened to their child?

Herr Minster drew the cart to a stop, pulling on the reins enough to get the single horse to listen. "Herr Kosner." He tipped his cap.

"Herr Minster." Wilhelm aided his wife in her descent, a needless accommodation for someone of preternatural ability but necessary to keep up the rouse that there were, in fact, no dark ones of any kind. "Lisi, did something happen? Where is…"

She laid a hand on his heart. "Jelena is in the back." She grimaced. "With her."

"Her?" Wilhelm turned to the loose hay in the cart, trying to see over the top into the blanket of pale yellow. His sense of smell did nothing to inform. Did the hay cover the scent? "Who?"

Just at that moment, his adorable little Jelena's head shot into view, bits of hay sticking out of her hair. "Hello, Papa."

Relief flooded his soul. "What are you doing back there, little lamb? And who is with you? Did you bring back one of Herr Minster's puppies?"

The children had been on him for two weeks, ever since Frau Minster had asked Lisi if the family would be interested in adopting one of his bitch's litter to "chase all those wolves people are always saying are up in those hills near you."

Wereolves didn't need dogs. Try telling that to the children.

Jelena's eyes went wide. "No, Papa, but I would love that an awful bunch. Jacob and I promise we'd take care of her."

"Lisi?"

The voice drew away Wilhelm's adoration of his incorrigible child and set his teeth on edge. The smile on his face melted, the need to use caution in the presence of laymen, dangerously on edge of being ignored. "Jelena, come down from there." Wilhelm pulled his wife behind his back.

Lisi swerved between her husband and the cart. "Wilhelm, hear me out."

"She cannot be here." His whisper came out as more of a growl. "She's Andreas's ma... An outsider."

"She is also days away from giving birth," Lisi shot back.

Wilhelm's eyes went wide, until he recalled that, indeed, enough time had passed since the day the wolfsretters attacked the packlands for a proper brooding.

Herr Minster, having maneuvered to the back of the cart, paused. "Frau Kosner, didn't you say this was one of those Faust girls?" He scratched his head and turned eyes on the ground. "Always thought they were a bit bluer than traveling by merchant caravan, but that's the way she came in. You sure we shouldn't take her up the hill? Her family would want to—"

Lisi turned on the laymen, pouring honey into her words even as she cut him off. "She married Andreas Baron, Herr Minster. You remember Andreas, don't you? My cousin, strapping farmer? I'm afraid the Fausts didn't accept the marriage and she and Andreas decided to find their fortunes elsewhere. But she's come back to stay with us..." Lisi carried her gaze over her shoulder to her husband, growling, "...at least until the baby is born."

Wilhelm crossed his arms and huffed. "Fine, then."

The males were the stronger in body of their species, but when it came to will, the bitch always ruled. Besides, it was never a good idea to infuriate the shewolf you shared a bed with unless you were eager to not share a bed with her.

Defeated, Wilhelm rounded the cart, expecting to find the Gerwalta he remembered from eight months before, only with a significantly larger waistline. As it turned out, he was to have his second surprise of the morning.

"Saints help us. What happened to her?"

The voice he recognized, but the face... He'd always thought of the youngest Faust child as mildly handsome, even if she were a wolfsretter. Ivory skin, bright, intelligent eyes, and apple red hair. The hair was still red, but everything was some disturbing color of black or blue. Only one eye looked up at him out of a face made dough, the other swollen shut. Her clothes were those of an everyday woman; no fine, imported, and costly fabrics here. Gerwalta was dressed like them: as a farmer would be. As Herr Minster reached down, Wilhelm did the same.

Gerwalta's black eye turned up on him. "I fell down."

If there was one thing Wilhelm knew for certain, it was that whatever misfortune had befallen Andreas's mate, that was the last possible truth. How did a creature who could fly become injured by a fall?

They were in trouble. On one side of the barn, all the members of the pack who believed turning Gerwalta over to the wolfsretters was best. On the other, all those who believed she should be given sanctuary until the baby was born, then turned over. On the former side, all the males of the pack. And on the other...

"If you give her to the red, the baby is as good as dead," Lisi surmised, her statement bringing nods from the shewolves. "You can believe what you like about Gerwalta, but her child is one of us and holds no fault for the misjudgment of its parents."

"It is only half wolf," Jacob Fitz, Lisi's brother, shot back from across the barn. "We don't know what it will be like. What if it cannot take fur? What if it doesn't heed the full moon? What if it—"

"What if it has horns and a duck bill and gobbles at the moon instead of howls?" Esther, Wilhelm's own sister, jumped in. "It doesn't change the fact that it is an innocent baby. We are many things the laity are not, but murderous of children for the sins of their fathers? That has never been our way."

Michael Fried coughed a laugh. "It isn't our way to give comfort to our overlords. The child is half wolfsretter. We'd raise a spy in our very midst. And what of the mother? How do we know this isn't some ploy to embed Gerwalta Faust—"

Lisi rolled her eyes. "Gerwalta Baron."

"Gerwalta Faust," Michael insisted. "The wolfsretter bitches don't defer to their husbands like our women do, and that is only one of the many ways in which they are different. It's unnatural, is what. Besides, you cannot tell me that you honestly believe she sincerely loved him. Then why did she abandon him and come here, half-dead and alone?"

"Because my mate is dead."

All the wolves shot to their feet as the ragged, swollen creature wrapped in one of Lisi's sheepskins hobbled into their midst. Her suffering made itself known by every twitch in her face with each step. When finally Gerwalta reached their throng, she dropped to her knees, her eyes trained on the floor.

"An interloper to my clan did this to me, all to get to Andreas, to drag him back here."

"Such manure!" Michael scoffed. "Why would a wolfsretter drag a convicted wolf back anywhere? Why wouldn't he just kill him where he stood?"

"Because it is easier to move a living body than a dead one," Gerwalta said. "My mother pursued us after we fled. She would have killed Andreas, only she discovered I was with child and it moved her heart. She... She cut off Andreas's hand, used it to claim the kill."

All the wolves felt it then: the shiver that overcame them when remembering the sliced-off appendage mounted outside the Schloss gate. They'd been told it was Andreas's but they refused to believe it but couldn't be sure. He was no longer of the pack; would they know if he passed, or would had those bonds been eternally severed?

"The wolfsretter from the House of Night captured Andreas to prove my mother's lies. After that, though..." The woman's face curdled like milk left to lay, tears streaming down over flushed flesh. "I tried to tell him. I said his love would kill him, and now it has. Andreas is dead, and it's all my..."

The words after that tapered off. Lisi closed in, wrapping Gerwalta in her arms, pulling her forehead to her shoulder. Wilhelm surveyed the room and found on each lupine's face the same reaction. Disbelief. Not in Gerwalta's story, for its plausibility melted well into the mold of their reality. Rather, it was for Gerwalta herself. A righteous wolfsretter, a daughter of the House of Red, openly weeping for one of their own. Openly showing weakness before a pack.

A wounded animal baring her injuries before predators inherently bent to hate her.

Gerhart, königswolf, cleared his throat, rising from the milking stool on which he'd sat listening. "I don't care whether this red-blooded pig lives or dies."

The shewolves bared their teeth, but Gerhart held up a hand, silencing them all.

"But her sin," he continued, drowning all the growls, "wasn't against us. A fact is a fact, however. She is the mate of an exile, and having left with him, accepted his punishment as her own."

"Don't be ridiculous," Lisi snapped as one of the other

shewolves came forward to assume her place. "Gerwalta didn't know that is our way. And what could she have done if she had? Would you have let her stay with us as a packling?"

"Of course not." The king's tone bordered on anger. "She is not, cannot be one of us. I do not wish the child harm. Believe me, I do not. But I am king, and as king, it is my duty to protect this pack from threats of any nature. A child who could very well turn the power of the enemy on us from within... That isn't a risk I am prepared to accept."

Lisi's face went red. "You cannot be suggesting that..."

"Enough!" Gerhart spun. "It is their nature. Even when their heart softens... Look at what happened to Andreas!" he barked, letting the second woman go. "Their hate burns, but their love poisons. I won't have this among us. Wilhelm!"

The second, roused from observation, stepped forward, even as he examined from a sideways glance if his mate was well. "Yes, mein könig?"

Gerhart waved a hand dismissively. "Take this traitorous whore to the Matron. She isn't our bitch to whip."

"But she'll die if you—" Esther barked.

"Enough!" Gerhart spun, his chest puffing, his eye bulging, his voice full of brimstone. "This is the king's command! Now, Wilhelm, obey!"

Wilhelm looked once at his wife, then to the king, and at his wife again.

It was all very good for Gerhart to spite Lisi, but it would be Wilhelm who'd be sleeping with the pigs come morning.

TWENTY-ONE

As Zelda's feet slammed the stairs of the wall leading to the gate, Gerwalta closed her eyes against memory. How distantly in the past it seemed now, that day when Gerwalta herself rushed to defend the Schloss from the intentions of the königswolf. How could she have known then what fate had in store? If she could go back to that day and refuse her mother's orders to accompany Andreas on his mission, all this could've been avoided. If she had asked to join in her cousin's conspiracy when it had been discovered instead of killing him over it, she'd be far from here, perhaps raising a child already. A child whose legitimacy wouldn't be questioned by her clan. A child whose birth wouldn't bring so much death.

Zelda grinned. "My, my. What have we here?"

Wilhelm cleared his throat. "Frau Faust."

"Herr Kosner." Zelda surveyed her bruises and cuts with mild disinterest. "What a pretty present. But she looks somewhat... used up. What happened, did the pups have some fun with her?"

Beside her, the wolf bristled. "Frau Faust, your sister is weary and beaten and days away from giving birth. Show some compassion."

So the pack's second had been on Lisi's side of the argument? How interesting.

"Shall I just kill her right here then?" Zelda pulled the lever that allowed the gate to open. "If only the Matron hadn't said I'm not to harm her should she show up."

Gerwalta stepped forward, a prisoner being transferred, until her body jerked back.

"I don't care what Gerhart says," Wilhelm spoke into her ear when her back pressed against his shoulder. "You chose one of us over all of them. Die with honor, die without fear. Die like a wolf."

His words warmed in a way she hadn't expected any to. "Thank you, Wilhelm, but I knew where this road led when I set out on it. Give Lisi my thanks, tell her all is fine."

"How can you say that when they mean to kill you?"

Gerwalta took two steps forward. "Because I've no fear."

The gate slammed back into place the moment they were through, and even though she could no longer see him, Gerwalta felt Wilhelm's tenderness as they crossed the outer and inner bailey.

At midday, the hall stood empty. Her family and most of the servants would be upstairs or in the other buildings of the complex, sleeping away. Zelda shoved her sister down on the floor of the throne room, using a pair of iron shackles to secure her to one of the ornate pillars.

"Wait here in silence, or I'll make you wait in the dungeon while you scream."

She needn't ask wait for what. Gerwalta knew. The Matron. Not her mother who, no doubt, was condemned and overthrown the moment Andreas had been revealed to be alive, but for Helga, who at this hour would be in bed, high in the tower in the Matron's chambers.

Water dripped in some distant corner, reverberating off the stone walls. Bells rang in the valley; their song crawled up the steep hill. Her bladder disobeyed commands and emptied itself beneath her. Nothing to be done for it, unfortunately. A mouse squeaked as it passed, pausing to sniff her toes. She proved even below its interest and it skittered off.

She shifted, her bones aching. As a nascent, she'd been trained to keep her body under her command, to separate the physical from her consciousness. Pregnancy had made her both wonder at the body's capacity for change, but it also made her feel like an outsider in her own skin. Even now, as she attempted to ignore the way pain shot up her back and down to her toes, she hoped the suffering proved worthwhile.

Suddenly, feet pounded up the hall. Sound became sight as Gerwalta, eyes trained on the floor, noticed a pair of pointed slippers come to a halt on the ground before her.

"Well, well..."

Pain shot through her body as Helga fisted her hair and yanked Gerwalta's head up.

"Little sister," Helga hissed. "What big eyes you have. What big ears. What a mouth. Every part of you is as swollen as that hideous gut of yours." Gerwalta cried out as Helga whipped back her neck. "Someone has had a go at you, haven't they?"

"I suspect he had a go at you as well." Gerwalta's soft words still lacked no courage. "Mehmet's scent is all over you."

"Is it any sin for a Matron to share a bed with her husband?"

"Husband?" As much as her swollen eyes could allow, Gerwalta squinted. "But I killed Alexandre."

"Ah, an open admission of one of your many crimes." Helga petted her sister's matted red hair. "Not that I needed it, but it does make killing you a little more... defensible."

"Kill me if you wish," Gerwalta spit back, "but spare my child. Our law has no sanction to execute a child, even if it is born of one of us and a lupine."

"Do you think that matters? No righteous wolfsretter would allow such a creature to survive."

"The House of Night would," Gerwalta said.

Just then, Mehmet strolled into the throne room. "Oh, I'm sorry, Gerwalta," he said, taking a position at Helga's side. "That's actually not true."

"But... in Venice, on the ship. The lupine and her mate, the asenaic..."

"What asenaic? Ahmet was a stupid wolfsretter who raped a lupine. A sick thing, really, that mating bond of theirs. Made the shewolf fall in love with the man who forced her innocence. Don't worry, he was properly punished after we parted. After that, she saw no point in going on and took care of herself, saving me the work."

"But you said that... I sensed another wolf. I..." Terror struck at her as the tie of the deception loosened in her mind. "She was pregnant. The wolf I sensed and sometimes didn't sense... It was a baby." She looked up at the interloper with angry eyes. "So she's dead."

Mehmet leaned down and stroked one of his long, bony fingers down her cheek. "That's what I do to betrayers. I kill them. But you?" He shook his head. "That beating I gave you in Navarre should have killed you both. I stabbed you, but even that didn't work did it? Here you are."

How could she not have seen from the beginning what a loathsome creature he was?

"My question is why?" he said instead. "It isn't to save your mother, and you must have known we'd kill your mate after he served his purpose. So, tell me then, Gerwalta, what was it that forced you through all that pain and suffering, just to have more pain and suffering?"

All emotion drained from her face. "I'm here because he is my mate, and because I cannot live without him."

Helga leaned in, bringing herself inches from Gerwalta's face. "Don't worry, you won't have to." Then rising, she turned to Mehmet. "Take her to her old chambers and lock her inside. Tonight, her bones burn with the wolf's."

TWENTY-TWO

Gerhart hadn't been a bad königswolf, but that didn't mean he was a good one either. He didn't, for example, ask for an invitation to enter the bedroom after giving one gruff knock.

"Lisi Kosner!" He growled her name like an insult. The king burst in, his cheeks red, his chest puffing. "What is the meaning of this?"

Lisi finished folding one of her son's shirts and placed it into the sack. "The meaning of what, mein könig?"

"Don't treat me as a fool, woman! Every mother in the packlands is readying their children for a journey, all saying that you are the one who gave the order." The king took two more steps forward, planting his pointed finger into her chest. "I am king. I alone can order the children the leave the farm."

"You've no argument from me, your majesty," she mocked. "I ordered nothing. I merely told the mothers of the pack and only the mothers that I was sending Jelena and Jacob into the forest for a few days with my sister and invited any who wished to do the same to have the children ready by twilight. No one is under any obligation to—"

"Don't you think I see what you're doing?" Gerhart interjected. "You're going to try to free Gerwalta, and where will that leave me? There's no way you and a few other lunatics can take on the whole Red clan!"

Lisi placed the sack on the foot of the bed, next to a nearly identical one she'd packed for her daughter earlier. "There are more members of our pack than there are wolfsretter in the schloss. With Gunda Faust in the dungeon, Gretchen serving in Ravensburg, that leaves only four in the castle. Both the Matron's father and brother are on patrols, and they'll pursue a group of juvenile wolves breaking off from the packlands more than they'll worry about any of us."

"And all four can draw a blade or arrow of silver into existence in a blink and kill you dead," Gerhart countered. "Is that what you want, Lisi? To send the children back and have them return orphans? And for what? To rescue a wolfsretter?"

"I would never put my life in danger for the likes of Gerwalta Faust, but the baby she carries... It is an innocent pup, Gerhart, one that sadistic Helga will take much joy in torturing before she finally kills. Even if Andreas has been exiled, it doesn't mean we can stand idly by while the Reds destroy his child."

"But how can you justify risking the shewolves, the mothers of this pack, to save one bastard child?"

"Because the child is a lupine," she answered. "Don't tell me you didn't sense it, smell it when Gerwalta was here."

The king's façade began to crumble. "I won't sanction war against the wolfsretters."

"My intention merely is to force a negotiation to free the pup and only the pup whence it is born."

"And just how would you negotiate?" Gerhart asked. "It is full moon! Yes, our lupine strengths will be at their greatest, but all of you will be unable to reclaim your skin. You'd need a king with you to serve as mediator."

"I agree," Lisi said. "My question now is, will that be you, or must I ask Wilhelm to challenge you?"

The king wolf recoiled at the mere suggestion. Wilhelm was a beloved son of the pack, one they'd known for years and respected. Second to three kings, and while a mild soul, capable of vicious animalistic terror. In short, a foe not to be easily trifled with.

"He will do it if I ask it of him, and he will win. Do you know why? Because his love for us in his strength, while yours is only hate. The only reason you won against Andreas was that he was so desperate to lose," Lisi said. "You know you'd never have defeated him otherwise."

An inferno raged in Gerhart's eyes. "Is that what you think? Well, then, we shall see, won't we?" He turned toward the door. "You have your wish, bitch. We are going to the Schloss. And there, I will kill

Baron once and for all."

TWENTY-THREE

Gunda had never felt sympathy for a wolf, and the emotion didn't fit well. If she had silver, she'd put Andreas Baron out of his misery. Or perhaps, put herself out of her own.

"Must you make so much noise?"

"I am going moon mad. I can feel it." Andreas's bloodshot eyes rolled her direction. "This is how I end. The full moon comes and I am bound in silver. My body is driven towards fur, but the metal repels my ability. My mind cannot take it."

It had been an act of cruelty to hold a wolf prisoner. When Helga had visited towards evening, wrapping a layer of blood-claimed silver around his bonds, she'd become the devil herself in his eyes. With the rise of a gravid moon in the midnight sky, every bone and muscle in the wolf's body broke and tore, only to fall back to his layman form again and again and again. Add to that the fact that the silver also burned away large portions of his flesh, and there was no wonder how much he suffered.

"I'm going to die without ever seeing my child." The wolf let out a jagged sigh as his eyes turned back to the ceiling. "How will he go on, when I am gone? Who will care for him?"

"My daughter, your wife, of course," Gunda snapped. "Or do you think your mate unequal to the task?"

"No, but... My child needs a pack. He needs..."

They both stilled their tongues when the dungeon gate flew open and a shadow of a man paraded in. Apart from his olive skin, everything about Mehmet was black. His cloak. His eyes. The hair and beard that helped conceal his features in the dark. His heart. His soul.

His ambition.

"Matron."

Gunda hated him. Not because of the kind of person Mehmet Siyah was, but because he represented every quality she had tried to instill in her own children. Each had fallen flat on some key criteria, and only now she managed to be thankful for that. In his wake, her second-born daughter Zelda and her husband, Helmut, followed. Zelda pushed a key into the lock of Gunda's cell, letting the door swing open.

Mehmet reached for the link of the chain that kept Andreas secured. "Hungry yet, wolf?" he asked, pulling Andreas to his feet. "I do hope so. It's time for your last supper."

When Andreas opened his mouth, more moans than words emerged. "Kill me if you will, but I won't die a murderer."

"Oh, I think you'll find yourself more tempted than you might suppose," Mehmet said.

"Mother." Zelda swooped in, taking a key to the chains tying Gunda to the wall and unlocking them.

"Don't call me mother, you foul child. Not when you've forsaken me like this."

"Very well, then. Gunda," Zelda corrected. "Recall your cloak."

Fisting folds of red fabric, Gunda took a step back. "What?"

"You won't drag your bloodline down as you die. Disrobe and go to your death without clan."

"But I…"

"Now!"

Zelda's tone allowed for no margin of disagreement. Gunda took one last look at her arms, her tunic, imagined herself reaching back and throwing the hood over her head. Then, she closed her eyes, and made it disappear, leaving her only in the soiled, laymen-made garments.

She hadn't truly felt defeated until this moment. But like the wolf and she agreed, what did it matter, when you were about to die?

"Finally." Zelda tugged on the chain, pulling her mother along.

At first, Gerwalta didn't understand what she was seeing. It was almost like when she was a child and her father shaved off his beard. It amazed her that the man she'd called Papa and played with every day could suddenly look like a different person yet be the same. It was the first time Gerwalta could remember seeing her mother without her cloak, and it didn't pass her over how much smaller it made the woman who had loomed so large in her memories. In the outer bailey, her mother had been tied by all fours, outstretched on the ground. She was a skeleton that merely clung to its meat.

Gunda's weary head rose, catching sight of her daughter. The Matron's stony resolve ebbed into sadness. "In the end, it was all for naught."

"Walta!"

Gerwalta spun and felt all the wind rush from her lungs. Andreas, bound in silver chains, no doubt blood-claimed to prevent any attempts at heroics, fell to all fours when he saw her. At first, she thought because the moon was pulling him inevitably towards his fur. Only then, she realized that as high as the moon was, he should already be in it. The horizon bisected the sun, but it was dipping fast. The full moon already had begun to claim the sky.

"Walta, fly! Go!"

She shook her head. "I cannot."

His face went suddenly blank. "Then we are all lost. Ah..."

"Silence, dog!" Mehmet's foot landed square in Andreas's ribs.

"No!" Gerwalta pulled, lunged, strove, but Helga's restraints proved too strong. With every effort, all she gained was frustration, until Helga slackened the iron chains, letting her fall to the ground.

"Oh, take heart, little sister," the new matron cooed as she kneeled at her side. "You'll survive the night. You see, I've decided that you shouldn't die alone. I'll let you hold your baby to your chest when I burn you. But mother..."

At that moment, the statement was broken up by Andreas's tortured screams.

The sun had disappeared.

"Withdraw the silver!" Gerwalta begged, her open palm slapping down on the packed dirt. "You're destroying his mind, keeping him in flesh like this."

Helga just laughed. "That's the point. A few more minutes, I think, and then, when he's nearly mad with the effort, we'll let him loose on Mother."

"You heartless, cruel, bi—"

But Gerwalta never got the word out. It was cut short by her own groan as her body seized and a spasm wrenched her.

The smile on Helga's face evaporated. "How very convenient."

Zelda, standing nearby, spun. "What is?"

Before Helga could say anymore, Gerwalta cried out again. How was it possible? This couldn't be the baby coming. A first delivery took hours if not days. This pain had come from nowhere and was already akin to the worst of what she'd seen her sisters go through.

Zelda swooped in, bracing her arms under Gerwalta's and lifting her to her feet. "She shouldn't deliver for several weeks, at least. I don't have a birthing chamber prepared."

"Fool, her child is half-lupine. Their waiting time is less than ours. Of course this baby would be born sooner than a wolfsretter."

As Gerwalta's screams erupted for a third time in as many minutes, she was joined by Andreas.

"It is your own blood!" he shouted across the bailey. "You heartless beasts, how can you treat your own blood like this?"

"I'll do what I can in the time we have to prepare." Zelda began to move Gerwalta back toward the castle.

Gerwalta did what she could to plant her feet. "Please, if you won't let me say goodbye to my husband, at least let me say goodbye to my mother."

"What cause, little sister? You'll both be dead come morning."

"Then what cause to oppose?" Gerwalta mumbled. "Please, Zelda, you are a mother too. Would you deny your daughter this?"

Zelda's expression soured. Sucking on her own lips, she turned her eyes to Helga. "Matron?"

Bit by bit, Helga's muscles tightened, until finally, she huffed and took Gerwalta by the hair, pushing her down to her mother on the ground. "Make it quick."

Gerwalta paused only a moment to nod at Helga before crawling close to her mother. "I want you to know, I forgive you."

"Gerwalta, I—"

"Shhh—" She wrapped her hand around Gunda's where it was tied to a stake. In an instant, her mother stilled and her eyes went wide. Gerwalta leaned in to kiss her cheek. "I send you my love. Do you understand?"

The relief of leeching the silver off her skin lasted only a moment as Gerwalta felt another convulsion come on. She fell forward, her fingers digging into the earth.

"Take her away!" Helga commanded. "Mehmet, cast the chain so you can take shelter inside, then release the lupine from his bond. We'll return to kill him as soon as he's killed my—"

The orders stopped as Gunda unbound rose to her feet. "You don't mean me, do you, daughter?"

The new Matron fell back to see her predecessor on all fours, a silver sword in her hand. `

She pulled back the weapon, ready to take on any who would dare approach. "I raised you better than this. If you want me to die, you kill me."

Gunda grinned. "The moment I touch the silver, it will obey me. I am Matron. Remember, Mother, you brought this on yourself."

Then, everything seemed to happen at once.

Helga charged. Gunda swung. Gerwalta called out. Mehmet pulled back the silver chain, forcing Andreas to howl.

And the pack?

They poured into the courtyard from every direction.

TWENTY-FOUR

With all her focus on the executions at hand, Helga had forgotten the most critical part of being Matron: to protect everyone not a wolf from everyone who was.

That included the wolfsretters.

Fur flew in every direction, driving the ill-prepared House of Red to the edges of the courtyard. Outside of the chain made of Mehmet's blood-claimed silver, no one had a supply upon their person. No one, it seemed, except Gunda.

At least that means the wolves will target her first, Helga thought.

"Everyone to the keep!" she called out, waving her hand and running for the doorway.

"Helga!" Mehmet tugged back on the chain, even as Andreas Baron phasing between his two forms in dizzying succession pulled and writhed. "Help me. I cannot come through them."

Helga pushed the last of her clan through the schloss door before turning one brief moment to lock the black-cloaked figure in sight. "My name is Matron."

No sooner had she turned than the wolves reached Mehmet. The chain fell to the ground, and its form lost definition as he pulled it all in, sheltering his body from both fang and claw.

Finally, Andreas could take his fur. And that would allow him to take his revenge.

Never but in her worst nightmares had Gunda imagined the

scene before her. Her family fled, closing the door to safety, closing the door on her. All around, wolves driven to fur by the moon encircled. On the ground beneath her, Gerwalta clutched her rebelling body and called out for her husband through the pain.

The wolves had followed the fleeing parties as far as the door, but the moment they were out of sight, they refocused. It didn't take a wink for them to surround her, all circling, the pack moving like water, bearing fangs, growling, but awaiting their king's order.

What to do? She could fly herself to safety; of that she was pretty certain, but would the wolves protect Gerwalta or destroy her? Carry Gerwalta along? Impossible. As much as the pain was causing Gerwalta to thrash about, the feat would prove too daunting and dangerous. Surrender to the wolves and hope they showed mercy? Why would the creatures she'd spent her lifetime subduing and oppressing show her a kindness? And even if they at least came to Gerwalta's aid, Gunda was no fool. Her family hadn't really fled; they'd retreated to gather weapons. It wouldn't be long before Helga led a charge back into the courtyard, silver at the ready, to destroy them all.

"Stay back!" Gunda threw herself over Gerwalta, brandishing the sword. "I'll kill any who comes for her."

At least if the wolves fell upon her, she'd die fighting and she'd die quick.

No sooner had the words left her mouth than the new king-wolf approached. A massive beast, black fur with a brown undercoat, looked poised to kill. Gunda leaned in to whisper into her daughter's ear. "If you survive this day, run as far as you can and carry my love with you wherever that is."

The king snarled, Gunda shouted, and they both lunged. They hadn't reached each other, however, before they were both knocked back into the ground. Gunda shook away her confusion as she pressed callused hands down, pushing herself up.

Andreas Baron, his lupine form far stronger than his mortal one had looked, stood sentry before her.

His body ached. His heart pulsed. His mind vacillated between man and beast. But this he knew... the king and his pack were here to save the child, but they weren't here to save Gerwalta. In fact, with labor under way, assuring Gerwalta's welfare wasn't even necessary. Lupine infants had come into the world from dead mothers before. Even werewolf women died in childbirth. If Gerwalta didn't survive... Well, then, there was a way to free the babe, as gruesome as that was.

Man.

Beast.

Man.

Beast.

The beast within demanded that he protect his pup. The man longed for his wife. Both Andreas's natures agreed, however, that either outcome demanded proximity. With bounding leaps, ignoring both the agony of a body beaten bloody and the torment of a mind poisoned by silver, Andreas had crossed the bailey. A ring of wolves, all his old pack led by their new king, surrounded his bride and, to his surprise, Gerwalta's mother. Gunda could have saved herself if she wanted. She could fly, after all. Had Gerwalta not gone into labor, perhaps she could as well. One look at the fierce pose the former Matron struck told him, however, that Gunda had no plans to sacrifice her daughter to allow for her own escape.

But Gunda couldn't protect Gerwalta and take on Gerhart. Andreas would save Gerwalta, then, but the best chances for that success would be greatly aided by saving her mother first.

The pain ebbed and Gerwalta finally opened her eyes. For the last several moments, she'd been blind, relying on nothing more than the sounds around her. She knew she was surrounded by the wolves. She knew her mother was near. She'd known her clan had fled the courtyard.

They'd return with weapons. She understood this, because Gerwalta had never stopped recognizing what a realistic outcome would look like. She'd known from the day she'd run off with Andreas that it was the first step towards her own death. She never expected, however, that the path would lead back to her own front door.

To her husband and her mother, working together, to defend her against the wolves.

She pushed herself back as the melee ensued but took some relief in the fact that the pack didn't attack. Rather, the battle seemed only to be between Andreas, Gunda, and Gerhart the King. Why were the other wolves waiting? Why didn't they join in? Why weren't they falling collectively on her, who had backed herself unprotected against the wall?

Then it hit. Because the king was fighting with an intention to kill, and Andreas refused to yield. Andreas was fighting back. Not just for her. Not just for their daughter. He was fighting to win back his pack.

And with the pack on their side, how could Helga and the others triumph against them?

"Mother, fall back!"

Gunda shook her head. "No, he'll be over—"

"FALL BACK!" Gerwalta repeated. "It is a challenge. Let Andreas fight." Let him win. "The pack awaits the outcome, and the magic cannot happen if you interfere."

Gunda dropped her sword to her side and turned. "Why would he want to—"

"Because he's trying to save us both. He—"

A red cloak flew down from above, landing just behind her.

Helga's silver blade bit into Gerwalta's neck. "Fall back into the keep with me now, or you'll die before you can scream."

Broken, beaten, malnourished, and on the edge of madness,

Andreas fought like he'd never fought before. Perhaps because of the love he now had for another. Perhaps because the only alternative at this point was death.

Gerhart was a worthy opponent, but that wasn't a surprise. After all, he'd beaten Andreas before. But on that occasion, Andreas had wanted to lose. Tonight, he needed to win.

At last, the black-furred wolf yipped when Andreas's maw took his throat. Power surged through his body as the pack's loyalty shifted. Andreas didn't waste a moment. He turned just in time to see Helga pulling Gerwalta back into the keep at the end of a silver blade.

With one mighty yelp, the werewolves fell in behind him.

"Hurry!" Gunda Faust shouted as she joined the pack's ranks. "To the tower with Gerwalta, Andreas. The pack and I will secure the stairs so that no other may breach."

Helga drove forward but had barely managed the throne room when the wolves burst through the doors. She spun, the blade's point drifting away. Gerwalta saw Helga's hand outstretch and threw her weight forward. Her teeth dug into her sister's soft flesh, drawing blood. Drawing temptation.

Fresh meat. Fresh kill.

The silver blade clanged on the floor, its ding bringing Gerwalta from her hazy bloodlust just in time for another pain to bend her in two.

"Animal! How dare you?" Helga called out, pulling her bleeding hand into her chest. "Now, you die!"

Gerwalta fought past the pain to reach for the blade. The moment her finger brushed it, the locus of her agony shifted from her center to her limbs. She flopped unto her back, using her feet to push her body away from Helga's approach, knowing it was no use.

Helga salivated as she reached her feet, her silver staff drawn from reserves painted against her person. She lifted the instrument back in the air, and then... fell back as two wolves moved into attack.

Gerwalta had no time to react. Before she could even manage to roll onto her side, someone had their arms braced under her shoulders from behind and was pulling her to her feet.

"We make for the tower!" he said.

"Andreas." Joy. Utter joy. "You defeated Gerhart. You are king."

"And you, my queen." He kissed her forehead as he swept her up into his arms and began to cross the room. "Our little lamb picked an auspicious moon to be born under, didn't she?"

Gerwalta laughed. "You finally admit it's a girl."

"I pray that it is, so she can be every bit the shewolf her mother is."

At the base of the tower, Gunda stood. "Hurry!" she waved them on.

Andreas came to an abrupt stop. "There are no stairs."

"Gerwalta will make them of the silver that sits there." Gunda pointed at the large metal disc of a floor that surrounded a central pillar.

The wolf gently placed his mate on her own two feet. "She can't. The silver doesn't listen to her now. It burns her."

Before Gunda could get a word of question in on that, Gerwalta stepped into the stairwell. "I'll make it listen, even if it kills me."

Gerwalta fought her own body, even as it broke and betrayed her. Her knees turned to dough, her heart became a drum in her ears and her sex. One hand shot out, bracing the wall, steadying as much as she could. The other encircled the shifting, bulbous belly she'd watch grow for the past eight months.

Not yet, my love, she begged of the child within. Just a little longer. Just let me get to the top of the tower.

But the ruined wolfsretter was to learn her first lesson in motherhood: it isn't the way of things for the child to obey the parent.

They were almost there. A few more steps, and they'd be safe. Andreas held her up as another labor pain struck. Or it could have been that he held on for his own support. Wolves didn't favor heights, and Gerwalta fought with all her strength to keep the stairs solid beneath her feet.

"Walta?" he yipped.

"I... will... not... let... us..." The seizure gripped her, her womb constricting, driving fire into her gut, crushing her determination. Gerwalta doubled, pushing her hands out in front of her, catching the edge of the steps.

Andreas breathed a sigh of relief as the stone landing held them up. He stopped on the stair above, turned, blanched. He was so gaunt, so unnaturally wane and weary in a way she'd never seen any other lupine. Gerwalta had never known a werewolf had the capacity to become beleaguered, but that had been before she and Andreas had been forced to flee, running the length of God's green earth just to keep their own lives. He pulled Gerwalta to her feet. Or tried, for the pain still held her captive, and even her strong will proved incapable of resistance.

"Walta, please," he begged, gently coaxing her. "Just a little more, my love. We're almost safe."

Her words were more cries now than voice. "I'm coming."

The wolf found her a shade of white lighter still and assumed it, even as he whisked them into the first room he came to: the Matron's bed chamber.

"I am sorry, Walta. This will hurt."

Without warning, her husband managed to heave her up, pulling her into her arms, even as the bolt of anguish sunk into her again.

"Andreas!" She squeezed shut her eyes against the suffering, seeing red without the benefit of sight.

"A moment more, love. And... look, we are here."

Gerwalta took what relief she could from the cool sheets beneath her thin, torn frock. Andreas knelt at her side, pushing pillows drenched in her sister's scent under her back. "I don't know what comfort I can offer but ask it of me and I'll do what I can."

"Just promise me that you'll do whatever it takes to make sure our child survives."

The lupine wrapped her frail hand in his paw, drawing Gerwalta's white-knuckled fingers to his lips. "I swear to it."

The tender moment passed as the ache of labor lit her body on fire. Gerwalta dropped Andreas's hand, planted her palms flat against the bed, threw her head back, and screamed.

"The baby is coming."

These words not from either of them, but from a third who had just entered the room.

Andreas teetered on the edge of shifting. "If you try to hurt her now, Matron..."

"Cease your fight, cursed wolf!" Gunda Faust snapped, even as she closed the door behind her and worked to move what heavy items the room offered in front of it. "Do you think I fought beside you below just to kill you up here. Now, step aside, unless you know how to birth a baby. Guard the door. Helga will make her way here soon enough."

The emotions cycled through the lupine's face. Anger, spite, frustration, and finally, acceptance. "If another member of your clan enters this room, I'll tear them limb from limb, just, please, protect my pup."

The Matron sat on the bed, wrapping Gerwalta's hand in her own. "When the pain comes again, push."

Gerwalta shook her head as the tension ebbed. "The labor just started. It cannot already be time."

"Wolves' pregnancy is shorter, and their labor quicker still. Prepare daughter. You're about to experience the worst pain you've ever felt, and the quickest ever forgotten."

No sooner did the words fall from Gunda's lips than the pain came upon her again. Gerwalta bit her lip, biting down so hard, her teeth were soon stained with blood. "There is something wrong!"

"All mothers think so, but a child is a miracle, and those come with no small amount of sacrifice and pain."

Gerwalta lashed her head side to side, grunting her words. "No... something... is... wrong."

Gunda softened, rubbing Gerwalta's knee as the contraction tapered off. "I'll look. Try to relax. I promise, I'm not going to hurt you." She lifted the frock, discerned the situation, and lowered it again, giving Gerwalta a smile. "All is well. Now, I need to gather something to swaddle the babe in. Breathe."

Gerwalta was either too weary to hear, or too trusting to answer.

Gunda stood, catching the unspoken attention of the wolf. She waved him aside, out of Gerwalta's earshot. "The baby is breach."

"What does that mean?" Only, then, he passed into an expression of resolve. "It matters not. I'll love her, no matter what she is."

The fallen Matron exhaled frustration. "Breach means the baby is turned the wrong way, and I fear that Gerwalta has already pushed her into a place where I cannot correct it."

"So you're saying..." The wolf's eyes verily spun. "What are you saying?"

"I'm saying that you have a choice to make, Herr Baron. I can save your daughter, or I can save mine, but I cannot save both."

Suddenly, the choices balanced on the end of his tongue. "How? Gerwalta is my mate, what is my life without her? But my daughter is pack." He looked up, the weight of the world in his eyes.

Gunda wrapped a hand over Andrea's shoulder. "You are a

king, Andreas. You need to make a king's decision. But truth be told, it may be too late for my daughter. The look of her..." She bit back a tear. "I know what death looks like when it creeps into a woman's face. But your child could survive." She turned somber eyes on the wolf. "If you are willing to make the sacrifice."

In short order, the Matron explained the plan and left the fate of all in the werewolf's hand.

His eyes closed in the wake of his decision like the axe of the executioner. "I know what I need to do then."

Gunda nodded, prayed for the Almighty's forgiveness, and set about her task.

TWENTY-FIVE

It took nearly an hour for Helga to gather enough silver from around the castle to form the stairs and make her way to the top of the tower. Gerwalta had retained the customary pool at the top, an attempt to delay the pursuit. That's all it had done, however. Delay. With her bow staff in hand, she led the charge up the stairs.

Gerwalta would pay for this. Never before had one single wolfsretter committed so long a litany of crimes. Mating a wolf would have had her sister exiled, but this? Her body and baby would be sliced into steaks and roasted over a fire and fed to the dogs. Her bones would bleach in the Black Forest until the end of days.

Each step mirrored the anger rising within her. Kill the wolf, cut the baby from my sister, rip Gerwalta's heart from her chest. As to her mother, Helga could go either way. If Gunda submitted, she'd gladly offer her a quick, painless death at a more convenient time. But if she got in the way... Both Alexandre's and Maria's graves testified that Helga was willing to do what was necessary.

In the tower, Andreas wore more blood in lieu of clothing. He sat on his heels, looking at the carnage staining his hands, rocking back and forth. On the bed, Gerwalta stared, glassy-eyed, in Helga's direction. Something about this didn't make sense. Why wasn't he running? Why wasn't she crying out? Surely Gerwalta must know this was the end for all three of them. And where was their mother? Had Gunda fought to bring them to safety so hard just to abandon them at the first opportunity?

Then Helga relaxed her eyes, taking in the larger picture. Gerwalta's tan frock was stained red. Certainly birth came at the price of some bleeding, but this was... This was...

This was more than birth. This was death. Gerwalta's body was practically torn in two.

Helga took a step back. "You... You killed my sister."

"Shh!" Andreas Baron pushed a crimson-stained finger to his lips with his one remaining hand. "You'll wake the baby."

A curl of sickness worked through Helga's gut. She took survey of the room. "Where is my mother?"

"Dead." The corner of the wolf's mouth ticked up.

"But how did you..." Suddenly, Helga put together the clues. So much blood. More than one person's? "You ate my mother."

"Yes, and I must say, wolfsretter is far sweeter a meat than even I imagined. But I found one that is sweeter still." He pushed a finger into the edges of Gerwalta's ravaged corpse. "Had to claw at it to get to it, though."

The statement landed on Helga like a physical blow. She'd been prepared to kill anyone who stood in her way, but seeing this before her... Even her stomach turned. "You've gone mad."

"No, Frau Faust. I'm actually quite clear, perhaps the clearest I've been in months. Your scheming and treachery cost me everything. My pack, my bride, my home... I wouldn't let you have my child. She rests now with her grandmother." He tempered a laugh. "In the belly of the beast."

Helga threw a hand over her mouth to stop the revulsion of her innards. "You ate your own daughter?" Even her iron constitution threatened to break at the thought. "If one ever needed proof of why we are necessary to your existence, you've given it for centuries to come. You are truly a monster."

"You say that, but all you had to do to prevent all of this, was love your sister and your family more than power. But if you think, now that I've gotten a taste for your flesh, that I would stop, then—"

But he never got to finish his sentence, for Helga had had enough. The eldest daughter of Gunda Faust breathed in her power, and breathed out her revenge, driving the blade on the end of her staff deep into the lupine's heart.

Blood bubbled on his tongue as the eerie smile stretched across his face. Andreas managed one last, longing look at the dead woman on the floor before him, then turned his eyes up to his slayer.

"Thank you, Matron."

TWENTY-SIX

She needed to fly, but not yet. From the top of the mountain with the vantage of the schloss, Helga or the others need only look out to see her figure darting across the moonlit sky. The moment Gunda had been able to make the ground, she did. Then, it was just a question of how fast could her feet carry her.

Gunda tried to remember the last words her daughter and the lupine had said to her.

"When you come to Navarre, find Igor, the vampire you knew as Goran Karahan. He'll take the child and keep it safe."

Andreas Barron had looked down at his daughter, and she could see all the lupine's strength engaged to keep from crying. Even she had problems not weeping. She didn't care what happened to the wolf, but she was a mother. To know that you'd never see your child again, that you'd be gone from this world and rely solely on the best intentions of others to raise it and keep it safe...

"But why would a vampire raise a child born of a wolfsretter and a lupine? I could raise her. I can keep her safe."

Andreas smiled. "You'd try. I know you would. But both lupines and wolfsretters will want her dead. She is safe with neither. I had hoped that..." His chin dipped. "It doesn't matter."

"Very well, then. I'll take her to Karahan." The sounds of feet pounding up the tower steps told them time had run out. "Quickly, give me the babe and do what you must. I... I cannot watch it be done."

What kind of mother could? Even if it created a story that Helga would all too readily buy and keep her from thinking the baby survived, inducing her not to look for it, what kind of mother could watch her youngest child be ripped apart by a werewolf?

The vampire looked at the bundle in his hands, then up again at Gunda, then to the bundle again.

"They told me you could be trusted. They said you would care for it."

"I..." Karahan's words cut off as he broke into a smile. "Did they say why?"

She shook her head. "But I would ask you to do more than that. I would ask you to kill it."

His eyes snapped up from the child. A wave pulsed through his face, pushing away his amusement. "Why would you come so far, protect it, spend up all your silver to procure the services of wet nurse after wet nurse, all just to bring it to me and ask me to do something you yourself could have?"

"Because she is my blood." Gunda fought back the tears, fought back the exhaustion threatening to topple her. "And I will not... cannot force myself to do it. Andreas and Gerwalta entrusted me because they thought I would have mercy enough to bring the baby to you to raise. But I've more mercy than they realized, because I know how a child born of our two lines can find harbor in neither. There will be no place for her in this world. I thought that you might consider..."

Karahan closed his eyes. "I would never kill a child," he growled. "I would never take the life of an innocent."

"But she could never..."

"She will!"

Gunda jumped back, the wave of his anger a physical blow against her body.

"She may not have a place with wolves or hoods, but I am neither of these things. I'll protect her from everything, even your bigotry and hopelessness."

Gunda nodded, lowering her arms to the side. "Then I've done what I came to do. I'll leave you, Herr Karahan."

"Not so fast, Frau Faust."

The wolfsretter paused in the doorway.

"What you ask of me is no small thing, and while I'll raise Gerwalta's child as if she were my own, it isn't done solely out of the kindness of my heart. You will need do something for me."

She turned, her chin buried in her chest. "Yes, Lord?"

"The silver jars holding my own errant sons," he said, "I retrieved them from Schloss Wolfsretter when I understood you had interlopers in your house. They aren't safe with me, however. My longevity makes it necessary for me to restart with some regularity. I cannot be responsible for relocating the jars with each move. Vlad wasn't without his supporters, and they will use those times of readjustment to free him if the jars if I did."

"And how could I aid that?"

"By taking them and putting them someplace safe."

TWENTY-SEVEN

Zelda wiped the last of the blood on to her cloak as she took a place at Helga's side before the unlit pyre.

"Everything settled?"

Zelda bobbed her head. "The surviving wolves have been rounded up and expelled back to the packlands. Wilhelm Kosner is the new königswolf. He has been detained to bear witness."

Wilhelm? Yes, that would work very well indeed. He'd been Andreas Baron's second, then Gerhart's. He was used to taking orders and doing as he was told. Oh, and Helga would be giving orders and demanding obeisance for some time to come. The pack had to be punished for their insurrection. Had she a choice, Helga would've ordered them all killed. They deserved it, for certes. But even a new Matron understood that little power was gained in death. She'd fortify her rule better by allowing the pack to live but making the legend of their oppression one that wouldn't soon be forgotten. She'd raise her own daughter to be a matron every bit as cruel and ruthless as well. It would be her legacy. Ten generations from now, the pack would still be suffering for this revolution.

"Bring him into the courtyard after we've mounted Gerwalta and Andreas's bodies onto the spits." She pointed at the silver structure she herself had created. Burial was too dignified a process for such traitors. The order was passed back into the schloss even as Helga continued. "Speaking of which, are they almost ready?"

"Helmut is putting the corpses unto the litter now. It is funny, though..." Zelda's voice tapered off.

"I doubt anything regarding this is funny, Zelda."

"No, of course not, Matron. My apologies. What I meant was, it is peculiar," the third-born daughter amended. "Are you certain the wolf claimed that he ate the baby?"

"You saw the way Gerwalta's body was left in shreds. A child was ripped from that womb by force, I have no doubt of it."

"But, Matron, we found the babe still intact."

Helga spun. "What?"

"A little boy," Zelda said. "He was dead, of course, though I cannot say if that was because of something that happened before Gerwalta died, or if he simply suffocated in the womb afterward. His hand slipped out from the visceral when Helmut moved her body."

Helga bit her tongue. If the child had in fact not been clawed out of its mother, then what was the wolf playing at, saying he did?

If only the dead could speak...

"The child is dead then? I am agreeable to that. Light the pyre. I want the first thing Wilhelm Kosner to see when he emerges is me, standing before the spitted, burning body of his fallen king. I want that image seared into his brain so deep, it is still fresh on the minds of his great, great grandchildren. Let no packling or member of our clan ever forget: it is a crime for a wolf and a wolfsretter to love, and death to all who break this sacred law. None goes unpunished."

Helga watched as the flames grew hungry, burning through the fuel. And when the fire reached the smallest of the three bundles atop the pile, she smiled.

None goes unpunished.

None.

THE STORY CONTINUES...

The consequences cascade through the centuries, as truth is obscured and the name Gerwalta is struck from the lips of the wolfsretter...

...until it is at last passed on to new member of the House of Red. In the modern American midwest, "Geri" Kline tries her best to outrun her namesake's shadow and her own mother's strict expectations and live by her own rules. It's not long, however, until she comes to the aid of a lone werewolf in the streets of Chicago. Soon, Geri finds herself stuck between vampire conspiracies and werewolf warfare, and discovers the very thing that may save her is her link to the past and her infamous ancestor.

THE RED CHRONICLES is a complete urban fantasy series that expands on the world of RED ORIGINS, taking readers on a exciting ride through supernatural society. See if Gerwalta "Geri" Kline can save the day, save the wolf, and save herself from repeating her infamous namesake's mistakes.

Published by: Tulipe Noire Press

Text Design by: The Last TK

Cover Design by: Mario Lampic

ISBN-13: 978-1-733-76555-8

www.ingramcontent.com/pod-product-compliance
Lightning Source LLC
Chambersburg PA
CBHW060332260626
47160CB00007B/2781